The Worst Holiday Ever!

Imelda Megannety

The worst holiday ever!

For my ten grandchildren young and older, especially my amazing granddaughter Nell, who supplied the alien idea.

Chapter 1

The plane took off smoothly and nine children travelling with their parents tried to relax and not look back on another trip they had all made, years ago. They were younger then of course, and most of the horror of what had happened then had blurred and become a faint memory. Still, it's impossible to completely forget being in a plane crash and surviving a terrifying trek through a jungle. The great thing was, they had done just that. Now they were setting off for a different holiday, far from tropical jungles and they did not expect any hairy adventures, so, all was well.

Their granduncle Marcus lives in Bari, which is in the south of Italy, and they were going to spend some time with him on an 'educational tour', and then the plan was they would all head to Greece for a lovely holiday in a wonderful, rented villa, complete with their own pool.

Their parents were very excited about the tour that Marcus was taking them on, the children less so; they were a little bit suspicious about the 'educational' bit; that would hardly be fun, would it?

Mira, Rose and Bella were sitting together on the right side of the plane, the middle row had Liam, Faith and Nonie; the left side three seats had Hughie, June and Alfie.

Once they were airborne the chatter started and soon became very animated and loud. They had lots of things to talk about; school and recent trips and their pets and films they had seen and books they had read; they happily talked their heads off until lunch was served. After that, they felt a bit sleepy and dozed or played on their tablets.

The eight parents behind them all chatted quietly, then dozed off after lunch.

They were travelling from Ireland where three of the families lived. Bella and her parents Naro and Finn were on holiday from Australia, and this was the tail end of their holiday.

The weather had been cool, and damp and they were looking forward to a bit of sunshine, or rather, lots of sunshine. They were travelling in 'off-peak' times as the summers were now too hot to go on holidays to southern Europe.

Now the plane began its descent and suddenly Nonie got a bit panicky.

'I'm scared, Faith, please hold my hand,' her voice was barely more than a whisper and was very wobbly. Tears glistened in her large green eyes.

'Hey, don't be afraid, everything is fine, Nonie.'

Faith held the younger girl's hand and could feel her trembling beside her.

'Just think about the great time we will have in Bari; Marcus has about seventeen dogs now and we will be going for pizza on the rocks tonight.'

'I'm gonna have octopus every day I'm here,' Liam said, 'what about you, Faith?'

'Ohh, calamari, octopus and then more calamari and of course, pizza.' Faith quite liked octopus and calamari and so did her sister Mira.

'Oh, I don't know if I'd like that,' said Nonie, distracted by the thought of eating something with eight legs.

'Never mind, there will be lots of different things to have; whatever you happen to like, Nonie.'

Faith had successfully taken Nonie's fear away and before they knew it, the plane had landed without a bump.

The next hour was extremely busy, gathering luggage and then looking out for Marcus at the exit. They had been warned not to bring too much baggage and they didn't.

There was Marcus waving wildly with a big smile on his face. He was hard to miss, with his bald head. After all the hugs and kissing, it was time to head outside to the two minibuses, one which was being kept idling by Monica, Marcus's other half, as he called her. Then it was all aboard for Bari, with Marcus driving the second minibus.

Their tiredness was quickly forgotten, and they talked non-stop as they travelled.

Monica was subject to a blitz of questions about how many dogs and cats they now had, and could they come to the kennels to see where they were voluntary helpers? They hardly gave the woman time to reply.

Chapter 2

The hotel was only ten minutes from Marcus's house, and it suited them all perfectly. After leaving their backpacks there, they were ferried by minibus to the pizza place down by the shore and happily munched pizza for the rest of the evening, while Monica outlined the trip, they would make tomorrow.

The nine kids did not pay too much attention as this was the educational part and they could only imagine the sea and sand and playing together.

They were so tired from the excitement of flying and so full of the delicious pizza, they literally fell into bed and slept soundly the whole night through.

The next morning was spent locally exploring the old town of Bari.

'Actually, it is quite interesting, isn't it?' Liam asked them all.

'Yep, I like it a lot.' Nonie was impressed.

'Imagine Saint Nicholas' bones are here in that basilica, that's amazing!' Faith and Mira had been unbelieving at first to hear that the original

Santa Claus had ended up here, his bones having been stolen from Turkey way back in the mists of time.

'Saint Nicholas is the patron saint of Bari, you know; many people are called that name or different varieties of it, just like in Ireland you hear the name Patrick, Pat or Paddy.' Marcus was happy to fill them in on all the details of his adopted home.

Then it was back to his house and time to see all the dogs he had accumulated through the years of working as a volunteer at the local kennels.

Hughie and Alfie were mesmerised by them all, plus the large number of cats that were kept in a separate place. Then it was time for Mark to feed his many animals and that took a good hour and a half. The visitors all left to return to their hotel, with plans to meet up later.

It was hot and very sunny, so after they had lunch at the hotel and a short siesta, they finally got to swim in the turquoise waters. It was like being in paradise, they thought.

'Can we have pizza tonight again?' asked Alfie as they got dressed a couple of hours later.

'Oh yes, please,' chorused the others.

'Well, Marcus has arranged for us to go on a trip to a city called Matera, not far away. He said we would enjoy it very much as it is unusual, and we will stay the night there.'

That sounded exciting to all nine kids, and they discussed what they would need to bring with them. It was so hot that pajamas were not needed; they would sleep in their shorts and tee shirts it was decided.

They left for Matera by local bus, and it took two hours to get there. Now they were really hungry, and wanted to eat before sight-seeing, which suited the adults. Everyone enjoyed a delicious seafood pizza or pasta; they all chose different dishes.

They joined a group of tourists, and their guide took them off walking, explaining the different things of interest. The adults were all deeply interested and asked questions. The children were by now just a little bit tired; it had been a long day.

June and Nonie were getting a bit weary now as were the two younger boys.

'Oh, I wish we could just stop walking,' moaned Hughie, and his brother nodded glumly.

'There is just too much to see here,' Mira said, 'we'd need a month of Sundays to see and explore properly.'

Then the guide pointed out their next destination: the Old Town.

The tour guide droned on and on; 'Matera was one of the oldest cities in the world, inhabited continually by different empires and peoples, occupied by Roman, Germanic tribes and others.'

The kids yawned.

'The first people here were cave dwellers also called troglodytes, who lived in all the caves here.'

Now the kids all became more alert. "Troglodytes"? Wow! Now that was interesting.

They heard then that the caves had been lived in up to quite recently by very poor people, living together with their animals, in horrible conditions: no electricity, running water, sanitation, resulting in disease. The poverty was dreadful.

Eventually the government moved all the people living there out, into houses, but now with renovation, the same caves had been transformed into very attractive and comfortable rooms for tourists to stay.

'Oh, I hope we are going to stay in a cave, tonight,' pleaded Nonie.

Alfie and Hughie were not too keen on that idea. 'What about electricity?' Alfie asked.

'What about toilets and baths?' asked Hughie.

'I don't care! It will only be for one night after all,' said Nonie and then June and the others agreed. They could rough it for one night, couldn't they?

'We'll appreciate the hotel in Bari all the more when we return tomorrow,' Rose said wisely.

Finally, the guided tour ended, and the group entered a café for much needed refreshment. Walking is such thirsty work.

Then they learned the exciting news; they would be sleeping tonight in those caves they had heard all about.

The nine kids all shouted aloud 'YAY' in joy, and gave each other high-fives.

Chapter 3

They looked around in wonder at these cave 'rooms', which had all been carved by hand, centuries ago, out of the rocky mountain.

They were silent in wonder. Imagine all those people who had once slept and lived all their lives here! It was awe-inspiring.

Alfie and Hughie were so impressed they forgot their fears. Why, this was super, there were proper beds and sinks with running water! For a moment only, they were a bit disappointed that everything was so normal, after all they had heard.

The parents were on a separate floor in a separate area, and wondered if the younger kids would be alright. The older kids assured them that they would be well looked after. Even so, Alva asked her boys if they would prefer to stay with them in their 'cave' room.

'No, Mum, absolutely not. I want to be able to tell my friends about this and write a story about it. We must take lots and lots of photos.' Hughie was now excited about the prospect of sleeping in a cave that had been slept in by troglodytes and animals. What an adventure!

All the rooms were slightly different, some smaller, some more angular, a few a bit bigger.

After some time, they decided which beds each one would occupy. Hughie was between Liam and Alfie; Nonie was in the next cave with June and Faith; Mira, Rose and Bella occupied the next cave.

For a while they were too excited to settle down and visited each other's rooms chatting and planning the next day's adventure.

'We have until five o'clock to explore the place and then we head back to Bari.' Liam told them.

'Yes, I think I heard Marcus say he was planning to do a barbeque.' Hughie smiled all around and Alfie gave the thumbs up sign.

'Is it the next day we take the ferry to Greece?' Rose asked, 'I sort of wish we had more time in Bari, to explore further. I would like to have seen those Trulli houses.'

'What are they?' asked Nonie.

'They are funnily shaped houses with sort of, conical roofs, built with granite slabs, which keep the inside very cool in summer.' Rose explained.

'I read that they were made way back, to beat the tax man, as they could be taken down in a jiffy when they heard the tax man was on his way to tax people with houses.' Liam smiled at them.

'When it comes to saving money and stopping the tax people getting it, they were on the ball.'

The two boys were nodding off now.

'Come on lads, time to sleep, we have had an enormous day and I'm bushed,' said Bella, stifling a yawn.

They all agreed and went quietly to their beds which proved to be very comfortable indeed, though being as tired as they were, they would probably have slept on the stone floor equally well.

The children fell into a deep sleep, and all was silent. The only thing moving was the small light outside every cave that cast strange shadows on the curved walls. At intervals the light seemed to move and quavered a bit, making the shadows leap and lengthen and almost seem alive.

After a few hours there was shuddering, and the lights suddenly went out. Now darkness was everywhere.

Alfie stirred in his sleep and moaned softly.

Then it seemed like a clap of thunder shook the caves and all nine kids woke simultaneously.

'What is happening?' Nonie was frightened and clutched Faith who was nearest her.

All were now out of bed and the floor beneath them seemed to be moving, as though they were on a boat.

There were strange and awful sounds all around them; the very walls and ceilings of the caves seemed to be groaning in agony.

They dressed hurriedly and shoved their belongings into their backpacks and gathered together outside their rooms onto the main passageway. One light bulb overhead swung wildly to and fro, giving only a dim glow now and then.

There were screams now and people shouting. The floor beneath them was definitely moving in a strange way and they had trouble standing upright.

They were all scared. What was going on?

Out of nowhere, there appeared a young girl, dirty of face and bare footed.

She grabbed Nonie's arm and started pulling her along the passage, jabbering in a language they did not understand.

Nonie resisted, but the girl was stronger and kept pointing ahead with her free hand, not letting go of Nonie for a second.

Liam thought he understood what was happening and felt the blood leave his face.

He whispered to the older girls, 'I think there is an earthquake, and we must get out of here-- fast.'

The older ones then hurried forward and grabbed the younger boys by the hands.

'Quick, follow that girl and Nonie, we must move fast.

Chapter 4

They stumbled blindly along the narrow and twisting passage, led by the girl and Nonie. Then they seemed to be going downwards, the ground was different, sloping and very uneven and the passage got narrower. After some time, the girl stopped and let Nonie's arm go. Standing with her back against the uneven wall she pointed ahead with her finger, all the time talking and nodding her head.

They of course could not understand a word she said but understood by her urgent voice and pointing finger that they were to follow this passageway.

'Veloce, veloce,' she sounded so desperate, that they knew immediately she meant, 'quickly, quickly.

Then she turned and left them, hurrying back, the way they had come.

They went as fast as they could in the darkness, feeling the sides of the passageway with their hands, not knowing what to expect next.

There was no time to feel afraid or to cry, the noise in the caves behind them was tremendous and they could still feel the ground under their feet moving.

On and on they went, blindly trusting that they would soon come to the end of this tunnel, for that is what it was.

It seemed like hours later that a glimpse of light could be seen in the distance. Gradually it got bigger and bigger and soon they could see the mouth or end of the tunnel and now they could run.

Gasping and sobbing they fled as fast as was possible with the heaving and uneven ground. The noise behind them was mighty; it sounded like a monster growling and roaring.

They just kept running, but some of the kids stumbled and fell and then they all had to just walk as best they could. They were too shocked to talk or cry.

Now they could see dimly around them, it was no longer pitch black. There was the sea ahead; they were on the beach! The waves seemed to be roaring too. Oh, the relief!

Only then were they aware of the throngs of people further down near the water's edge; hundreds of them, running, jostling and screaming and shouting.

They could see some boats near the shore and there were many, mainly small boats. Throngs of people rushed headlong into the waves to throw themselves into the boats. Men were shouting and pulling people aboard and it was all chaotic.

Then an awful thing happened; the sandy ground beneath the children's feet started to open and a deep chasm appeared. Nonie and the boys were pulled back by Liam, just in time.

Now the younger boys were exhausted, and Liam took Hughie on his back and Rose took Alfie.

They ran back and tried to find the best way to get to the water. It was then that June and Mira saw lights shining further down the shoreline, away from the throngs of panicked people. There they saw people waving and pointing to the boat that seemed to be lit up.

'Come on, lads, start running again, our only hope might be *that* boat, the crowds have not seen it yet.'

As they ran the screams and shouts faded behind them and the lights of the boat ahead got bigger and brighter.

At last, they were almost there, and the ground was no longer moving. Liam and Rose put the boys down, stretched themselves. It's not easy running with two boys on your back.

Now the shock was beginning to hit them.

'Where are Mum and Dad?' asked Alfie.

'How will we find them all in the dark?' asked Nonie tearfully.

'Look lads, we know there were hundreds of people back there and they must be among them, it was impossible to see.' Mira was worried but did not want any hysterics now. It was all out of their control anyway.

'We could not have stayed and started looking for them; the earthquake is still happening.' Rose being very practical offered her opinion, aware that it was not going to bring any comfort.

'I'd say all those people must have come from the caves and the people with the boats were the rescuers.' Bella felt sure this was so.

'Well, they didn't bring a lot of boats, did they?' June was not impressed by this 'rescue attempt.'

'How much notice did anyone have? Don't earthquakes just happen, out of the blue, or are they predictable?' Faith asked this question, but no one answered.

Their eyes were trying to make out the small figure beckoning them from a lighted doorway in the ship.

They hurried to this much bigger boat than the other ones they had seen, and it was brightly lit up. It did not look as if it were in the water, but just standing on the sand.

'Oh, thank goodness, we're saved!' said Nonie, and immediately burst into tears of relief.

Hughie and Alfie opened their mouths and started to howl too.

'Hush, lads, this is no time for hysterics, we must get on the ship and see if there are others aboard.' Liam took hold of the two boys' arms firmly and marched them up the gangplank.

The others followed silently, most of them hoping to wake up from this nightmare.

Chapter 5

The nine stumbled up the steps to the boat, which they now saw was surely a ship. Only now did the shock hit them and as they looked backwards, waves of sorrow and anxiety overcame them, and they all broke down and sobbed.

Helpful hands guided them into a sort of dormitory, and they sank gratefully onto the camplike beds and were asleep in minutes.

They must have slept for hours, probably because of the shock and the frantic running. When they awoke, they looked at each other fearfully and all asked the same question: 'did the earthquake really happen?'

Sitting up they silently thought about the previous night and then, realising it was true, most of them started to cry quietly, the younger ones sobbing loudly.

'Look, we are saved and I'm sure everyone else is too, so let's investigate a bit.' Bella needed to act and felt compelled to do something; it helped to subdue the awful panic she really felt.

The others looked at her dully and nodded their heads. Then they looked around their dormitory.

It was big enough to take a dozen camp beds, there was a small bathroom off it and a shower and toilet and wash basin.

They got up and started to prowl around softly. They could not hear any sounds of people outside. There were no windows to look out.

But they realised they were moving very smoothly and fast, they thought.

Faith went to the door and found it locked, which was very frustrating indeed.

Rose and Mira went and tried the door too. Then the three of them started knocking on the door.

'Hello, hello! Anyone out there? Can we please come out now?'

Nothing. Not a sound. They all looked at each other, puzzled but also uneasy. This was very strange.

After what felt like hours, the door suddenly opened and the nine rushed out, into another bigger room with a table and food on it.

This was more like it, they thought! Without hesitation they sat down and started to eat, realising for the first time that they were hungry.

Now they could feel the movement of their ship and knew they were headed home. Thank goodness!

Having eaten, they felt a lot better and relaxed and started looking around. Further down the room they could see what looked like portholes, so they all headed there to observe where they were going.

Something was very strange and odd; they could not see any sea, or water of any kind! The only thing visible were stars and lots of them, shining brightly in the blackness of the sky.

They were moving fast; they knew that as the stars flashed past them and other bright and differently coloured objects too.

Where were they heading? This was a ship like no other. They had all been on ferries while going on holidays and even when travelling at night, it was never like this.

Hughie and Alfie were mesmerised. 'This is a weird ship, isn't it, lads?'

The girls had no answer but knew something was not right.

It was Bella and Liam who guessed at the same time.

'It's a spaceship, no doubt about it.'

Everyone except the brothers looked horrified.

'We've been abducted by aliens!' whispered Nonie.

'Don't be daft, Nonie, there are no such things,' laughed Hughie.

Alfie was studying the faces around him and suddenly was not so sure.

'Are there aliens Liam? Bella? Rose?' He broke off as he saw the fear on his cousins' faces.

Hughie also became serious and worried. 'I always thought that was just made up; in comics and movies, you know?'

'I don't really want to be abducted by aliens,' whispered Nonie, 'I need to get home to Mum and Dad.'

'Don't worry, I'm sure we will be alright and get home soon.' Liam said this, not very convincingly. The truth was, he was scared stiff as were the rest of the kids.

'What are we going to do? Any ideas?' Faith for a moment felt like laughing her head off. This was too ridiculous; abducted by aliens!

June also felt a bit light-headed. 'Just let them come near us and we'll frighten them to death,' she laughed out loud.

Liam, Faith and Bella joined in her laughter, but it was more like hysterical laughter than real mirth.

'Yes, I'll do my kickboxing on them, just watch me! I have a medal and a cup for coming first, you know.' Hughie grinned triumphantly at them.

'They will be very sorry if they mess with my brother,' added Alfie, 'and I'll punch them in the belly.'

Now the other seven could not stop laughing at the brothers, they were SO FUNNY. Soon the room was ringing with really long, loud, raucous, laughter.

Oh, that felt so much better, there was nothing as good as a fit of laughter.

Then part of the wall slowly opened upwards, and for the first time they came face to face with their captors.

With horror, they realised that yes, they had been abducted by ALIENS.

Chapter 6

The nine stood open-mouthed and stared at the creatures before them. These creatures were staring open-mouthed at *them!*

There have been numerous pictures of aliens through the years and these creatures standing before them closely resembled them. The older children all had the same thoughts on seeing them; how did the world know what they looked like if they were supposed to be non-existent? Then they knew that somewhere at some location, they had been on earth and been seen or photographed. They were the same shape; triangular shaped faces and bigger heads in relation to their bodies, big bulging sort of eyes, if that's what they were, and strange bodies, if you could call them bodies; How could you describe their skin? It looked black but shiny and like plastic of some sort, but more solid.

They had two arms and hands, like humans; two legs and feet, but still they were different. They did not seem as 'bendy' as humans and their movements were stiffer and more like robots, the kids all thought.

Both species stared at each other, and the aliens started moving towards the kids, pacing around them and staring intently at them.

Suddenly Nonie started to giggle. She had seen strange looking creatures before, in caves in Ireland, called Ooglies. Compared to them, these aliens did not look so scary, she thought.

June gave her a dig in the arm and said "shush".

The aliens stopped in their tracks, and all crowded around Nonie. Now she was scared, and the giggles stopped.

One of the aliens put out a long finger and touched Nonie's mouth, then with both hands, forced it open.

After peering inside her mouth, he uttered strange sounds to the others, and they took turns looking into Nonie's mouth.

Hughie and Alfie now started to laugh, covering their mouths with their hands. Now the aliens swiveled towards them and examined their mouths. Now everyone was laughing, and the aliens looked confused and rather scared.

'Lads, I think this is the key,' snorted Faith, 'keep laughing, it's scaring them, they don't seem to understand laughter.'

Very soon the group of aliens left the room and the wall came down again.

The nine continued to giggle nervously until they gradually became silent.

Rose broke the silence by saying, 'now we have seen them, and they don't seem to be aggressive or hostile, what do we do now?'

'We must try and find out where we are,' Nonie muttered.

'What are our parents going to think?' June bit her lip, 'they will be so worried.'

'If they managed to get away from the earthquake area,' said Bella.

'I bet they are all back in Bari with Marcus,' Liam said this hopefully but was quite worried about it all. He did not want to cause panic by suggesting that they might still be trapped, or worse.

They paced around the big room, each wondering where they were and what would happen now.

The next meeting with the aliens took place a while later. They had no idea of time here; their watches seem to have disappeared as had their tablets and mobile phones. They felt very alone and very insecure.

The wall again lifted, and now they could see aliens going about their business, whatever that was. It seemed they were free to walk out of that room and they did.

They wandered around slowly and noted their surroundings. Next to the room they had been in, was a long wall with computers and all sorts of gadgets that gave out purring, squeaks and other strange noises. There was electric-like wiring all over the place, connecting the computers and other machinery.

At other tables sat aliens who all appeared to be working.

They gazed at the screens in front of them and at times tapped keyboards with their strange long fingers.

Liam and the older girls approached shyly and looked on.

'I wonder what they are seeing?' Liam said in a quiet voice to Bella.

Imagine their shock when a strange, robotic or a sort of electronically produced voice answered his question!

'We probe your galaxy to find answers to our mission, earthling, we understand many things but not all.'

'How did you learn our language?' asked Rose.

'We heard your speech in the rest room and have an appliance we turn on to translate to our understanding. It allows us to communicate with you.'

'Wow! That is amazing guys,' said Nonie. 'What language do you usually speak?'

'We seldom use sounds; we can read each other's thoughts; it is much faster than words.'

The nine were amazed at this. How wonderful to be able to read thoughts. This was like magic.

'Where do you live? On some planet, like us?' Mira was so curious and wanted to ask loads of questions, but did not know where to begin, or if the aliens would get annoyed with them.

'Yes, we have our own planet, and we travel a lot, picking up information all the time. There are so many galaxies and most too far away to travel to.'

'Is our planet Earth far from yours? Alfie just wanted to know exactly where they were and how far from home.

'Very far but not as far as some.'

Some other aliens were now standing beside the nine, listening to the conversation being carried out with the seated aliens.

'Why do you all look the same?' Hughie was studying them all intently.

'We *are* all the same,' came back the reply.

'Are you brothers or what? Do you have mothers and fathers?' Faith was getting quite daring.

'No, we are here always, we are not propagated like earthlings.' The alien who said this turned around to look at Faith and they could see that the alien regarded *them* as inferior.

Propagated indeed! Did they think they were vegetables or flowers? The older cousins felt indignant.

Chapter 7

The nine left the seated aliens and looked around at the other aliens moving about the room. They approached one who seemed to be staring at them a lot and smiled at it.

'Are they female or male? There is no knowing, is there?' Liam asked this of the girls as they neared the lone alien.

The answer came immediately. 'We are all same, not like earthlings.' Then the lone alien pointed to the girls and then at the boys.

'You different beings, we all same.'

This was a lot to absorb for the children.

'Do you have names, like us?' Alfie asked, looking up at this alien, who was not much bigger than himself.

The alien, who now became 'Loner', in the eyes of the children, shook its head, 'all same.'

Now it was the turn of the children to be examined, and that was not what they wanted at all.

An alien each took one of the cousins and started a strange examination.

On a sort of trolley, each one was laid out and hooked up to types of electrical lines, they thought.

This did not happen voluntarily. The older ones had pulled back and resisted but had then been gently prodded with a rod, that gave an electric shock. That caused them to become scared again. What were these aliens up to?

The examinations were not painful in any way; the electric lines did not hurt them, but they could see on the screen above each trolley, needles moving all over the place, and they wondered what they could be recording.

Liam thought they might be recording their heartbeats, or perhaps their brain activity. He knew they were gathering scientific information and was not too worried. If these aliens were hostile, they would have shown this earlier.

The two brothers were frightened and were quietly sobbing on their trolleys.

Their aliens leaned over and spoke to them: 'no need for this, little earthling, no danger here for you.'

This made the boys cry harder. 'We just..w..w.. want our parents,' Hughie sobbed.

'Yes, we are v..v..very lonely without them,' sobbed Alfie.

'What is "lonely"?' asked Hughie's alien.

'It's like, you know, sad and miserable,' Hughie tried to explain.

'Don't you ever feel sad and miserable?' asked Alfie.

'We don't do this thing, "feel", we don't understand this thing, that is why we examine you to find out what is different between you and us.'

Nonie, on the next trolley said, 'it's what humans do; they feel. You are not human so you can't.'

'Stop all this talk now,' another alien had approached, and they knew by his tone that they had better obey. This alien had a sort of rusty sound, as though his voice needed a bit of oil, so he was soon known to all as Rusty.

June was having her own problems with her alien. Her diabetic pump and patch were causing much interest and there was a small group of aliens now gathered around her, communicating with each other silently.

She was fed up with all this scrutiny.

'What is wrong with you? Do you mean to say that you don't understand what diabetes is? I thought you were a superior species!'

The other eight listened, terrified of June's tone of voice. She had a short fuse and did not suffer fools gladly. She was also quite an actress.

Rusty put up a finger to June and it really looked like what a teacher would do to a naughty pupil. 'What is this dia-bee-tes?'

June spent the next fifteen minutes trying to explain what it meant to the intent aliens.

Finally, Rusty spoke to June. 'This is very interesting to us, we need to know everything that can happen to humans or earthlings; you are very valuable to us, I think.'

Now there were nine very worried cousins. If they were going to be of value to these aliens, maybe they would not be allowed to leave.

Chapter 8

Back in the bedroom as they called it, the nine sat on their camp beds and reviewed the situation.

'They want to know all about us humans, don't they?' asked Hughie.

'But why? I don't trust them; I think they are baddies.' Alfie was still upset and nervous.

'I think they understand diabetes fairly well now,' said June, 'just as well there is nothing more complicated to explain.'

Liam pondered aloud. 'I wonder if they suffer from any medical problems?'

'Why don't we ask them more questions when they bring us out again. I'm sure they're not finished examining us yet.' Mira was worried. She did not like all this interest the aliens were showing in them. It reminded her a bit of the time they were lost in the jungle and met strange tribes, who were fascinated by the girls' hair.

Later they were again taken to the dining room where they had eaten before.

'Oh yuck! Looks like the same stuff again. They need a proper cook here.'

Hughie and Alfie both had their noses screwed up and the others laughed at them.

'Imagine being worried about FOOD! That's the least of my concerns,' laughed Faith.

'Well, I would not mind one of those yummy pizzas we had in Bari.' Mira sighed.

'Yeah, eating outside, sitting on the rocks, looking at the sea.' Rose sighed too.

The stuff on the table looked like it had come out of a packet. It certainly was not cooked or at least not freshly cooked.

'Never mind, we must eat, to keep our strength up. It must have some necessary nutrients in it.' Liam knew whatever happened, they must try and behave normally.

The nine ate the minimum amount of the stuff on the table that just took the edge off their appetites.

They thought with longing of the dinners that their mothers made. Their eyes became distant and dreamy as they thought of their favourite dishes; pasta, curry, chicken wings, fish and chips..... on and on they let their imagination wander, anything to take their minds off this TASTELESS stuff.

They left the table and wandered out into the main hall, as they thought of it, where all the computers were stacked against the wall, whirring and purring away, non-stop.

The one they called Lone, walked stiffly towards them, pointing to the dining room and then pointing to its mouth. Somehow the nine could not refer to any of these aliens as 'him' or 'her'.

Hughie and Alfie nodded, and Hughie said loudly, 'Yucky stuff.'

'Double yucky stuff,' said Alfie, sticking out his tongue and rolling his eyes, grotesquely.

The other seven started giggling and trying to stifle their snorts of laughter.

Lone looked at them and nodded, solemnly.

'Yucky, double yucky stuff,' he intoned in his synthesized voice.

That set all nine off, squealing with laughter. There were several nasal eruptions and they had to run back to the dining room to grab some paper napkins from the table.

Now they were surrounded by many aliens, who looked on, as the nine blew their noses noisily.

'Rusty came over and the others made way for 'him' or 'it' and was obviously the boss here. The nine thought Rusty was definitely a 'him'.

'Earthlings are ill?'

'No, not at all, sometimes this happens when we laugh too much,' explained Rose.

'Yes, it means we are very happy,' grinned Nonie.

'This brings feelings of happiness?' Rusty looked around at them all.

'Oh yes, we get lots of happy feelings, don't we?' Faith grinned around at them.

The aliens left them and returned to their computers quickly to type in this new information.

Rose did not think the aliens would be very impressed if they found out that the nine had been joking with them.

'They do not have a sense of humour, guys, just remember that; we don't want to annoy them!'

'Well, if they want to understand humans, they must learn about humour and feelings,' argued Nonie.

'We put the hum into human and humour, don't we?' Hughie said with a grin.

They all agreed that was true. Humour was such a big part of being human and so important.

Then it was examination time again and they reluctantly submitted to have their arm and leg muscles measured by a type of machine.

Lone was measuring Nonie, and she scrutinised the alien's face.

'Can I touch you Lo...', she caught herself in time. They do not go in for names, she told herself.

Lone asked Nonie what she meant by 'touch'.

'You are touching me with these machines, can I touch your fingers to see how they feel?'

'Feel? You humans must feel and have feelings all the time? You are a strange species.'

Nonie reached out and touched Lone's hand, then withdrew it hurriedly.

'Oh, that feels strange! I thought you were made of metal, but it's softer sort of stuff, isn't it? Stronger than the foil we put around the turkey at Christmas.'

'Turkey? Kissmas?' Lone now looked quite lost, his head on one side, staring at Nonie.

Rusty now appeared again, and it seemed to Nonie and those watching, that Lone was given a sharp look, for no words were exchanged, but as they all agreed later, 'if looks could kill, Lone was a goner!'

Then they were escorted back to their bedroom and were happy to lie down. They had no idea of time here, and wondered how long they were here on this spaceship. It was still moving fast. They had got used to the feeling of moving through space, rather like flying in a plane.

Soon they were asleep, dreaming of home and friends and family, and lots and lots of different food.

Nonie moaned in her sleep, as the image of a plate of potatoes appeared in her dreams, but they were behind a glass window, and she could not reach them.

Chapter 9

When they awoke, they again found food on the table next door and sighed as they saw the same Yucky, double Yucky stuff, as Alfie had called it.

The wall again was lifted, and Rusty and some other aliens entered and stood watching the nine.

Then Rusty beckoned them out into the main hall and led them to the computers. On the screen were numbers flashing on and off, then the screen would clear, and it seemed like it was filled with stars and objects that looked like planets. The older cousins could see they were nearing a planet; it was becoming larger and larger.

'Is this your planet?' Liam asked.

'Yes, this is one of our planets, we have many more, further away,' replied the robotic voice of Rusty.

'Do you have a sun and a moon, too?' Rose was so curious. She could hardly believe it was all happening to them.

'Not one sun, many suns and moons.'

'Wow, this is unreal,' murmured June.

'Not unreal,' rasped the voice of Rusty.

'Humans are not understanding our galaxy. Human galaxy so small, human brains so small also.'

'Huh!' snorted June. 'I bet you don't have cars and televisions and hospitals on your planets.'

'Or pizza parlours, or dogs,' said Hughie.

'Or tractors and trains,' put in Alfie.

The aliens all looked at each other and were obviously communicating by thought.

'Do you even have clocks and calendars?' asked Nonie.

'Clocks, we understand, but we have no need. What humans call Time is not needed here; there is no time here.'

'That's ridiculous,' snorted Faith. 'You are not really evolved yet; you are years behind us.'

Again, a lot of looks were exchanged between the aliens. Rusty walked stiffly away.

Liam was worried now. 'Faith, are you trying to get us banished into space? You are really annoying Rusty, and we must not do that if we want to return to earth.'

'I am fed up with Rusty and his mates and his yucky food. Who does he think he is? Lord of the Universe?'

Mira also got worried. 'Cool it Faith, we cannot afford to annoy them. How will we return to earth if they get angry with us? They could just push us off the spaceship into non-ending space.'

'We NEED them to get us back to earth,' reminded Bella. 'Please Faith, keep your voice quiet when they are about, will you?'

Faith walked away in a sulk. She went back to the bedroom and threw herself on the bed. She did not want to be here, she wanted to be at home in her own bedroom in her own house.

She was soon joined by Nonie, who felt the same way as Faith, but knew that the others were right. Faith needed cheering up, she thought.

Soon she began to sing a song. It was the one they sang when marching through the jungle, years ago, and had lifted their spirits a bit. This time she changed the words a bit.

'This old alien, he played one, he played knick-knack on my thumb....'

Very soon, Faith was laughing her head off and joining in the chorus, 'knick-knack-paddywhack, give the dog a bone, make those aliens send us home.'

The others soon joined them, and they all sang the song loudly.

Then the room was filled with aliens all watching and trying to analyse what these sounds meant. It was obvious to the nine that singing was not one of their talents.

The nine continued singing non-stop and the younger boys beat time with their feet on the floor. Soon they all felt a lot better, and the aliens departed in silence after observing them.

Chapter 10

The nine were highly amused by the alien's obvious puzzlement. How awful for them to live in a world without music, though.

'I wonder what they do to amuse themselves?' Nonie asked.

'Abduct earthlings?' asked Hughie, grinning around at them all.

'Not funny, Hughie, I want to go home,' Alfie was looking sad.

'They are not bad aliens, they are just doing research,' said Bella.

'But when will it finish?' June was fed up with all this.

'Let's ask them more questions, right? We should all ask different questions each time we are examined, and then we will discuss the answers we get.' Liam was thinking of the information they could gather about their abductors.

'Okay, we know they don't have feelings like ours, but there must be something that affects them in some way.' Rose was racking her brains to think of a solution to their problem.

The opportunity arose when the next examination came. They were herded into the exam room as they now thought of it.

Alfie was seated by Lone this time, and it appeared that his teeth were of interest. As he sat back on his trolley with his mouth held open, he decided to do a bit of examining of his own. His right hand sneaked out and he stuck his fist into the alien's stomach.

His wonder turned to horror as his hand seemed to go in for ever and met with no resistance.

Lone took his hand away from Alfie's mouth and he looked down at the hand that had pushed his middle inwards.

He looked a little uncomfortable and moved away.

'Sorry. Did I hurt your belly, Lone?'

Alfie forgot and called him the name they had given him.

'Hurt? What is 'hurt', is this another feeling?'

Alfie nodded vigorously. 'It is. When me and my brother fight, we sometimes get hit in the belly and it hurts.'

'Fight? You fight with your brother? Like make war?'

'Ah no, Lone, not anything like a war, just a thing that happens when he makes me unhappy or I make him unhappy, you know?'

Lone listened intently and did not reply.

'Please open the mouth again, just for a little look.'

Alfie obliged. He wondered if they had anything inside their bodies at all, maybe they only had a robotic brain in their heads and nothing else. Very strange indeed.

'Does your head ever hurt or make you uncomfortable?' His mouth was his own again and Lone was typing on his keyboard.

'My head?'

Alfie pointed to his head and then touched his own head.

'All electrical functions operating, always; never power-cut, like earthlings.'

'Do you eat food?'

'No need of Yucky double yucky here, we have all the energy required to exist.'

Alfie felt a bit disappointed with his information and wondered how the others were doing.

The girls' hair was proving interesting to the aliens now and they prodded and poked, pulled and measured the locks of all the girls.

'Ouch! That hurt,' exclaimed Faith who had very long red locks.

Her examining alien drew back a little and seemed alarmed by her expression.

'You should apologise for hurting me, you silly alien.' She rubbed her head which hurt, after the yanking she got.

'Hurt? Hair hurt?' Her alien then turned and communicated silently with another.

Now there were three aliens around Faith, looking and touching her hair, but gently this time.

'It's all good,' said one of them.

'No, you must apologise for hurting me.' Faith was stubborn and insistent.

'What is this word, 'apologise'?

'You must say "I am sorry for hurting you"; that's what we do when we hurt someone.'

'Does it stop the hurt?' Her alien asked.

'No, but it helps me to forgive you.' Faith said this with a grim expression on her face.

The other cousins were watching and were terrified of what Faith might do or say next.

'Please explain this word, forgive.' Rusty was now in the circle around Faith.

'Well, it just means that I won't be angry any more at what you did, because you are sorry. So now, you must say "I am sorry", understand?'

Faith looked at them uncertainly and felt a bit nervous for the first time. All attention seemed to be on her.

The aliens looked at each other, then they said in chorus, 'I am sorry.'

The cousins were left gob smacked.

Then Rusty led the group to the computers once more and they seemed to lose interest in the children.

They all heaved a sigh of relief. If only Faith would keep quiet and not make a fuss. They worried that it would turn the aliens against them.

Chapter 11

They later sat quietly after they had eaten the same meal once again. They silently thought about their experiences with the aliens.

Alfie related his action of pushing his fist into the belly of Lone, and how it had not seemed to affect him too much. 'It just went in and in, I could not feel anything at all.'

'They work on electrical impulses,' said Mira. 'My alien told me that.'

'And they don't need food. All their energy comes from the millions of stars.' Rose had found this out.

'Wow! Imagine that! They would not miss food at all then, would they?' Hughie mused in wonder at this information.

'No, we only need food for energy,' said Liam.

'Still, I'm glad we have food,' said Nonie, longing for a plate of freshly cooked potatoes, with butter.

'They only need to land on their planet for maintenance and electrical recharging.' Liam had discovered this information from his alien, who seemed happy to answer all his questions.

'I wonder when they are due to land again,' wondered Faith. 'I'd like to see their planet before heading home.'

This was met by a chorus of disproval. 'NO WAY, FAITH. WE WANT TO GO HOME NOW.'

'Yes, but wouldn't it be good to be able to inform people on earth about life on a different planet. We would be in demand by all the scientists. Joey would be jealous, wouldn't she?'

Joey was their eldest cousin and was studying Astrophysics. She would have loved to have been abducted like they were.

'You seem to forget that they have not given us any signs of wanting us to be returned to earth.' Mira said this sadly; they were beginning to feel that this was normal, and it most certainly was not.

'What are our parents doing now, I wonder?' asked June, 'and our friends?'

'Well, they would have no idea that we have been abducted, would they? There must be a lot of search parties for people after earthquakes. People will be searching everywhere for us.' Bella thought about the frantic activity that must be going on, back on earth.

Liam suddenly jumped to his feet. 'Remember they said that there is no time here? Well, I wonder if time has moved on at all, or if the earthquake is still happening on earth?'

'Time doesn't stand still on earth, silly,' replied Faith.

'Yes, but if there is no time here, then it's like we have just got on the spaceship, do you understand what I'm saying?' Liam was quite agitated.

'Yes and no,' replied Bella.

'It's too complicated for me to understand,' Mira said, and the others agreed with her.

They were tired again and fell silent one by one and finally slept their usual deep sleep. This time nobody dreamt of anything.

It seemed much later when they all awoke at the same time. Everyone sat up, alert and wide awake. What had woken them? Something was different.

Then an awful shuddering and shaking occurred and the nine were suddenly thrown out of their beds onto the floor on their backs. They were being flung around like toys and started screaming as they flew across the floor, continually passing each other and then changing direction and swirling around in circles.

'What's happening?' shouted Hughie as he passed Rose and June.

Then Liam collided with Bella, and she let out a scream.

'It's another earthquake! Oh, we're going to die this time!'

This was greeted by screams and cries of "OH, NO! NO!"

Then gradually, the swirling and shuddering movements became less and less, and now they were lying still on the floor. They lay there, holding their breath, afraid to move.

'We have stopped moving, haven't we,' said Hughie.

Yes, that was it! The violent movements had ended, but so had the normal movement they had got used to, everything had stopped.

The excitement became intense. 'We're home again,' shouted Alfie, jumping up.

They all rushed out to the dining room and found a porthole to look through. It was pitch black outside and they were disappointed.

Then there was a slight shuddering and unsteadiness as the spaceship rocked slightly to and fro and then seemed to settle, and now all the humming ceased and they knew they had landed somewhere, but where?

They all rushed into the main hall, or computer room to see what was happening there. The aliens were all gathered around the main screen and silently watching it. The nine could not get near enough to see.

Liam coughed, 'Excuse me, what has happened and are we back on the earth?'

He got no response at all. They were being ignored.

Nonie saw Lone outside the alien circle, he was also trying to look in. Shyly she approached him and touched him gently on his arm.

'Where are we, Lone, are we home yet?'

She did not care that she had called him by his name. He was unaware anyway of things like that.

The alien called Lone turned to Nonie.

'We have been struck by a big rock and it has spun us off course. That is what I understand.'

Then Rusty heard the conversation and turned to them all.

'Yes, earthlings, we have been struck by an asteroid and it seems we have been sucked into a black hole. Have you heard of these things?'

Well, they certainly had; their oldest cousin Joey was studying these very things and had tried to explain what they meant to the nine. Not they could fully understand this sort of stuff, not many people could.

'Is it serious?' asked Bella.

'Yes, things like this, are very serious, indeed,' Rusty was staring intently at the screen and the seated aliens were typing furiously on their keyboards.

Liam had heard a bit about black holes and knew that there were many theories about them.

'I have heard that there is a way to get out of them, we will not be stuck here forever.'

He looked around expectantly at the aliens but did not see any signs that they understood or agreed with him.

Mira and Rose talked quietly to the younger ones, who were getting a bit panicky.

'For sure there will be a way out; if there is a door in, then it stands to reason there will be a door out, doesn't it?'

Chapter 12

The nine understood that the aliens were taking all this seriously, as they had stopped all other activities to gaze at the big screen.

Rusty seemed to be giving orders, as there were a lot of looks exchanged and sometimes, he put his hand on an alien's back and pointed to various things on the screen.

'How will we start moving again?' Liam and Rose asked this.

'We need to recharge very soon, or all power will be gone,' one of the other aliens supplied this bit of information.

'Can't we use the gravitational pull to just drift off and when we get out of the black hole, there should be plenty of stars to get energy from?'

Hughie had read a book from the local library, about space and had a good grasp of things like gravitation.

Liam edged his way closer to Rusty. 'Have you shut down all the engines?'

'We keep trying to power them and there is some life, but not much.'

'I think you should really shut all engines off completely and conserve whatever power is there.'

'You want to shut ALL power off?' Rusty almost shouted this.

'Yes, turn it all off completely and then after a while reboot it.'

'Re-boot, what is this word?'

'It just means to turn back on again,' explained June.

'You earthlings think you can fix this?'

'Rebooting works for us when our computer acts up.' Alfie knew what he was talking about.

'How do earthlings know anything about our universe?' muttered Rusty.

'It's also OUR universe, remember. You don't own the whole of space, you know.' Faith was feeling belligerent again.

Rusty paused to look at her. 'Yes, but you do not have OUR brains, poor earthlings.'

'No, exactly! And you do not have OUR brains, do you, poor little aliens?'

Mira whispered and pulled her sister back. 'Will you please stay quiet, Faith, you will only make things worse.'

'Well, they think they are so superior, don't they? They just give me a pain in my….'

'Yes, yes, we know what you mean, but they are superior to us in this space world of theirs, aren't they?' Rose tried to placate the irate Faith.

'They would be at a severe disadvantage in our world, don't you think?' Bella whispered.

'Yeah, just look at their food,' muttered Hughie.

'And they don't even know anything about music,' added Alfie,

'Or dancing and singing,' said Nonie with a grin.

'Or mothers and fathers,' continued Faith.

'Well, they ARE different after all,' said Mira, 'we cannot expect them to think in the same way as us.'

'I wonder if we can help them find the way out of the black hole,' Liam said quietly.

'I was nearly going to say let's text Joey, but forgot we have no phones,' laughed Hughie.

After what seemed to the nine, like hours, Rusty approached them and spoke to the eldest ones.

'We are doing as you suggest, we will now turn off every engine and disconnect all things that need energy. We have tried all other options.'

'Good, it will help us, I am sure,' Liam nodded to Rusty. He was not at all sure if anything would work here; how could he? He had never been in space before.

They all gave a sigh of relief; it was important to keep trying and it gave them hope.

The silence descended on everything; there was not the slightest little hum of a computer. The aliens were all gazing through the portholes all around the main hall.

The nine returned to the dining room and looked through the portholes there. After a while they sensed a slight movement. It seemed that the spaceship was gently gliding forward, ever so slowly. It was not totally black outside, more like different shades of dark colours, black, grey, purple and in between shades.

Their eyes grew tired and soon the youngest three returned to their beds and were soon snoring.

The other six stayed staring and wishing for something to change.

Something did, but the six took a while to register what it was, their eyes were exhausted from staring.

'Look, there is a small light ahead. Can you see it lads?' June had her nose pressed against the porthole.

They all became alert again and now it was clear, the darkness was becoming lighter, but only a little.

They watched eagerly now, full of hope that they would soon be on their way again.

Gradually it got lighter and lighter and now they could see the usual stars.

They rushed out of the dining room to see if the aliens had also seen the change.

They obviously had, and there was great activity about all the computers, and the cousins could see that the screens were again lit up.

Rusty came towards them and pointed to the screens. 'Re-booted', and pointed to Liam and Bella, 'we are on power again, but must find our proper course.'

The six clapped their hands and all the aliens turned to see what they were doing.

'You feel happy, earthlings?' asked Rusty.

'Yes, we are VERY happy,' they all yelled back.

Chapter 13

Everyone was more relaxed now and eager to see if the spaceship was going in the right direction. They did not have long to wait.

In a short time, the aliens all started moving quickly about the floor, quickly for them, as they usually moved stiffly and not very fast.

The six stood silently watching and waiting.

They sensed panic in the aliens' movements, especially in Rusty and the more senior looking ones. Rusty moved from screen to screen, looking anxiously at each one before moving on to another. There was rapid eye movement between all the aliens and low synthesised sounds.

Bella stepped nearer and coughed politely, 'is anything the matter?'

Rusty turned and looked at them standing there. He looked at them as if he had never seen them before.

'Go earthlings, back to rest room, go, NOW!' He pointed his finger at them threateningly.

The six were alarmed. Rusty had never seemed so aggressive before. What could be wrong?

They trooped back to their bedroom, subdued and worried. The other three were still fast asleep and Alfie was snoring.

They sat on Liam's bed and asked each other what could all this mean?

'They should be happy, shouldn't they? After all, we did manage to get out of the black hole,' Faith sniffed.

'Yes, thanks to us suggesting rebooting.' Liam bit his lower lip. 'There is something bugging them, that's for sure.'

'It must mean that something is wrong, don't you think? Mira looked at Rose and both nodded.

'I'm afraid that something is wrong, too,' muttered June. Her voice sounded wobbly, and she was trying not to cry.

'There is only one thing that could have them bothered and that's being lost,' Liam said softly.

LOST? The five looked at Liam as if he were mad.

'They are used to travelling in space, silly!' Faith laughed.

'Yeah, space is their home,' Bella looked around at them all for reassurance.

Liam held up his hand. 'Let us not jump to any wrong conclusions. It is true that they live and travel in space, but coming out of a black hole may have changed things.'

'You mean the spaceship might have emerged into a different time or galaxy? 'Bella knew something like this might be possible.

Rose sighed and rubbed her forehead, then June started to whimper.

'If space is endless, and the universe is still getting bigger and time does not exist...maybe, maybe.... Liam's voice trailed off as he began to consider the implications of being lost in space.

The six were speechless after this, and a terrible tiredness descended on them, and they got into their beds and fell asleep very soon after.

Chapter 14

The three youngest woke first, full of energy and hungry. They left the others in bed and bounded into the dining room. The table was empty of any food whatsoever.

'Oh no! I'm really hungry,' moaned Nonie.

'Come on, let's go out and find Lone and tell him.' Hughie ran towards the hall, the other two followed.

Alfie found Lone first, he was, as usual, alone and working at the screen away from the others.

'Lone, we are hungry, we need food,' pleaded Alfie, pointing to his mouth.

Lone looked up, nodded and said, 'Yucky double yucky stuff?'

Three heads nodded enthusiastically.

Lone approached the wall where the biggest screen was and communicated with another alien. He was waved away, impatiently, it seemed to the three hungry children.

Lone came back and pointed to the dining room. 'Yucky double yucky stuff come soon.'

Hughie wandered off to see what they were all gazing at on the big screen. He could see what looked like lots of spaceships moving about in the blackness.

'Oh! Are they your neighbours?' he asked.

One of the aliens replied to his question, 'neighbour no, never neighbour, enemy. Want war with us.'

With this stark explanation, the alien turned back into the circle around the big screen, leaving Hughie looking confused and slightly worried.

The food appeared in the dining room as Lone predicted and by now the other six were awake and up. Even though it was the same monotonous food, they ate, because they were starving now.

Then Hughie related to the silent six his experience at the big screen and they all looked at him in disbelief.

'Enemies? Here in space? That's mad!'

June got up to look through a porthole.

'Maybe we were wrong about getting lost. Maybe we have strayed into enemy territory instead,' said Bella.

'Hush! Don't let the younger ones hear about our worries. We must try and pretend that all is well.' Liam was now very worried and was trying to pretend there was nothing to worry about.

The spaceship was moving although slowly and they could hear the familiar hum. They all looked through the portholes, but it still looked as foreign as ever; true, there were other objects like spaceships to be seen in the distance, but how near was distance here? There was no way to measure it.

'It's time we found out what is going on, this has nothing to do with their experiments on us.' Bella's chin was out, and all could see she was in a fighting mood.

All nine marched into the hall and walked up behind the huddle of aliens around the big screen.

'We demand to know what is happening,' said Bella in a strong voice.

'Yes, we want to know what is going on,' added Liam.

'NOW, this minute,' demanded Faith, standing with her hands on her hips.

'We need to go home,' pleaded Hughie.

The aliens barely noticed them. Their eyes were glued to the screen, and their bodies were all leaning inwards, barely moving.

Rusty held up a hand in the halt position, without turning around.

'Maybe we can help with the problem,' piped up Alfie.

Then Rusty turned and said in his robotic voice, 'Help? How can earthlings help when earthlings are the problem?'

'WE are the problem?' Faith stamped her foot. 'YOU caused the problem by abducting us!'

'Shush Faith,' said Mira. 'Why are we the problem, Rusty?'

'What is this 'Rusty'?' The alien looked at them.

'Oh, never mind, we just call you that because we must have names, you understand. It's in our tradition and civilisation to have names, you see.' Rose was trying to calm things down and thought she could reason with Rusty.

It seemed that Rusty had an answer to Mira's question as he led them away from the screen and into the dining room.

'We are not war-making, like the ones we are seeing on our screens, no, we are trying to save your world from these war-making creatures. They already know you are on our spacecraft and will soon demand we send you over to them.'

'You should not have taken us from earth if you knew they were waiting for us,' Nonie felt very let down by all this.

'No, we did nothing bad to *you*, did we? asked Hughie.

Rusty spread his hands in a human way.

'The only reason they have this knowledge is because we came out of the black hole into their territory.' Rusty looked at them as though he expected them to understand.

'Then we must try and go back into the black hole,' suggested Nonie.

'Not possible. We entered because of asteroid, now we here and lost.'

They all looked at Rusty in disbelief.

'We cannot be lost; outer space is YOUR world; you must know your way around it.' Liam was scared now; his fears had been correct.

Rusty seemed to slump and become smaller.

'No, we cannot know all of space, too big, never ending. Earthlings cannot understand; your world is so small.'

'If we managed to find ourselves here, then we can find a way out,' June said this confidently. She was beginning to feel sorry for this alien.

'You think this is possible?' Rusty looked at her.

'Everything is possible,' nodded Liam and the rest of the cousins all said in unison, 'EVERYTHING IS POSSIBLE.'

Chapter 15

The nine stood silently looking at Rusty and the rest of the aliens as they all rushed back to look at the screens in front of them.

'What did he mean, that those other guys know we are here?' Nonie was beginning to digest the information that had come from Rusty.

'They couldn't. How could they?' Hughie looked anxiously at Bella and Liam.

'I'm not going anywhere, except home,' said Alfie defiantly.

'Yes, just let them try to force us to go anywhere!' Faith was feeling belligerent again.

The others said nothing. They had a bad feeling about all this. Their own aliens were beginning to look quite normal, compared to these other war-making ones. However, it was obvious to them that Rusty and the others were frightened. It was a vibe they gave off; they probably would not admit to feeling fear, as according to them, they never had feelings, like humans.

'I'm hungry,' declared Nonie and so did June.

'Come on, let's see if there is anything to eat in the dining room.'

They were all tired now and automatically returned to the bedroom and lay down. They did not sleep, however. Each one went over the recent events and tried to figure out a way to get the spaceship back on course, or to get back home to earth.

'Earthlings, you must come out now. We must discuss much.'

All nine heads turned in surprise and found Lone standing at the bedroom door.

'Yes, you all come, now.'

The nine got out of their beds and walked in a line towards the computer area. They did not talk to each other; their thoughts were too busy.

Soon they were surrounded by a large group of aliens, all staring at them. Rusty stood apart and he seemed ill at ease.

'Well, what is happening now?' Bella asked.

'We have been commanded to send you to their vehicle, we will not be allowed to proceed unless they see you all first. There is nothing we can do, earthlings. We must obey.'

'Well then, you must DISOBEY,' said Faith in an angry voice.

'We must obey, it is the law of our universe. When they see you are only small earthlings, they will send you back here.'

'Small earthlings? What do you mean? We are children, do you not realise that?' Liam was red in the face.

'Yes, that is good, as they will understand that you are hopeless and know nothing about our universes.'

'Oh! Now we are hopeless and know nothing!'

Bella kicked the nearest object to her in anger, which was a type of table, then howled in pain. She had not realised how hard the material was in their furniture; it was metal, not wood.

'What are your feelings now, earthlings? Are you happy or not happy?'

They looked at Rusty in amazement. He thought they were happy.

'NO', they howled together, 'WE ARE VERY, VERY ANGRY.'

Lone approached timidly. 'No need for any feelings, all will be well, once they meet you. You will come back here and then we can travel away.'

Rusty came closer to them all. 'It must be done; there is no different path for us all.'

'How do you know they will return us? Maybe they will not keep their word,' whispered Mira.

'Yeah, I bet they all tell lies,' Faith said, but in a more subdued voice.

'Lies? What this word lies?' Rusty looked at her.

'It means, Rusty, that maybe they are not telling you the truth about what will happen us.' Liam looked at Rusty and hoped he understood.

'We only have true things here, not those things you say are Lies. They must obey also; they stronger but must obey the universal law.'

'Hmph,' snorted Faith, but Mira gave her a dig with her elbow.

'How and when must we go to their 'vehicle', as you call it?' Liam wanted all the facts now as it seemed they were powerless to do anything else.

'Their vehicle is coming closer, soon it will be beside us and you will just walk across to it.'

The nine all felt very frightened now and the younger ones held onto the older ones tightly.

Then all the aliens turned back to their screens and watched intently.

The nine kids moved forward and tried to see the screens. Lone came and beckoned them forward to his screen and they crowded around nervously.

They could now see an ENORMOUS spaceship coming steadily closer. It looked very intimidating compared to the one they were on.

There were so many lights glowing all over it, and blue flashing lights at the front, like a police car, they thought. The shape was different; it was triangular but in layers, as though there were many stories.

Now a huge fear descended on them all and the three youngest began to whimper.

'I want my Mum and Dad,' Alfie and Hughie both cried.

'I want to be at home, not here in this awful place,' cried Nonie.

The others wished they could cry but were unable to, the shock was too much.

Then the spacecraft came so close it almost touched and the humming of both ships stopped.

Now a big door was slowly opening, facing the side nearest to them; a covered canopy moved over the space between them, and then a platform pushed towards their spaceship like a gangway, connecting the two vehicles. Then Rusty said in his robotic voice, 'time for earthlings to cross over, come.'

Chapter 16

The nine children approached the open door of their spaceship with faltering steps. Their hands clutched the one beside them and slowly they crossed the platform that had been pushed into place by the other spaceship.

Liam was the first to enter holding Hughie by the hand, followed by Bella and Alfie. Now they were all standing in a large space filled with lights and humming computers.

Looking around them with frightened eyes they saw a very different-looking group of aliens. These were taller and looked as if they were wearing suits of armour, like soldiers in the olden days. They were covered in these silver suits just as their other aliens were all in black plastic-like stuff.

They approached the nine who were standing as still as statues. They walked slowly and stiffly like the other aliens. Their eyes were different, not those bulging things they were used to, but these were smaller and darted about quickly and seemed to see inside the children, or so they felt.

'Earthlings! We welcome you here and must ask questions before you can return, no need to feel fear.'

The one who spoke had excellent English and spoke of feelings! This was a change!

The nine suddenly felt a bit more relaxed, although still on their guard.

'Well, do you not speak?'

Liam swallowed hard. 'We do of course speak, but do you realise that we have been abducted, or kidnapped, from our planet? We all feel very fearful and want to return to our parents as soon as possible.'

'Yes, sometimes these things must happen. You are an alien planet to us and not always friendly.'

Bella felt a wave of rebellion. 'Not friendly? How would you know what real friendliness is? By abducting people?'

The others got frightened once again. What would the aliens do with this accusation?

Another alien came nearer. 'You think your planet is friendly towards us? Wrong! You have sent objects into our territory and littered our space with your rubbish and detritus.'

'What do you mean?' Nonie looked at the others and then at the aliens. 'I have never sent any of that D stuff or anything into space.'

'No! We recycle our rubbish,' June was indignant.

'We even pick up any litter we see, and put it in bins,' added Alfie.

The older ones thought they knew what these 'silver soldiers' were talking about.

'You mean things like the rockets the earth has launched into space?' Liam enquired.

'That's not us,' argued Faith, 'we are only kids and are still at school.'

'True, but this is what your 'so-called' civilisation does. Do you know that your rocket rubbish causes accidents here, just as asteroids and meteorites do?'

That thought had never entered their heads.

'That's silly! It all burns up when it enters our atmosphere; I have read that,' said Bella.

'Some might, but not all. Your rockets have crashed and caused damage and will continue to do this, so long as earthlings think they can dominate space.'

'Our scientists are very clever people; they would not deliberately hurt anything.' Rose was upset at the vision the alien had conjured up.

'Not so! They have much to learn yet. Your civilisation is divided; one nation trying to be better than another. With them it is just a race to be able to claim superiority, and they do not care how they do it.'

This silenced the nine. Never had they thought about this space race. It was true, they suspected; it was all a great competition to get there first and achieve the most.

'What exactly do you want with us then? We are not scientists; we have nothing to do with rockets.' Rose was beginning to feel desperate.

The 'silver soldiers' now came and formed a circle around the nine.

One of them walked among the nine, looking at them intently. Then he pointed at several and nodded to the others.

The ones he had pointed to, were now each taken by another soldier and physically pushed to another area of the room.

Faith, feeling her arm gripped in a vice-like hold, tried at first to resist, but it was impossible; they were just too strong.

'What are you doing?' she gasped.

'Some of you must stay. The others must go. Maybe the earthlings will pay attention if we keep you here.'

….'You mean, you are going to keep us here as hostages?' June wailed, and immediately was joined by most of the others.

Faith and the older ones looked like they might faint; the blood had drained from their faces and their bodies started to shake.

'I'm not staying without my brother and cousins,' sobbed Hughie.

Alfie was now crouching on the floor with his hands covering his face, too shocked to cry.

Chapter 17

Most of the 'silver soldiers' were now huddled over their computers and typing vigorously. The divided groups were still in the grip of the others.

Liam, Faith, Bella, and Hughie were in the group being held tightly. The other five were busy sobbing and holding each other.

Liam knew he had to keep calm and took a deep breath. 'This is very strange,' he said suddenly in a quiet voice.

'What is stranger than being here at all?' muttered Faith.

'No, really, do you not notice something?'

Bella looked at Liam, 'what do you mean?'

'Well, they have picked us four, one from each family. Do you not think that is strange?'

'Oh yes! It is, really.' Bella was puzzled.

'They couldn't know that we are from different families, could they? I mean, they are not THAT bright, surely?' Faith looked a bit scared now.

'I'm not sure about that; they seem to know an awful lot about us, don't they?' Bella began to feel a bit downhearted.

Hughie had been sobbing quietly but on hearing this conversation, he started to scream at the top of his voice. 'LET US GO, YOU HORRIBLE ALIENS. WE WOULD NEVER DO THIS TO YOU.'

His holder shook him, 'you don't know that; *your* planet is not as civilised as we. Your people do terrible things to others, such as we would not do.'

'Oh yeah? Like what?' argued Bella.

'You drop horrible things called bombs on each other; always you have done this.'

'We are not responsible for that,' Liam said quietly 'you know that we are only kids.'

'Kids grow into bigger human people and become like what has gone before them.' His alien relaxed his grip a little bit on Liam and Liam sank to the floor, holding his sore arm.

Bella covered her ears and started crying. 'I don't want to hear any more of this, I just don't.'

Rose and June rushed over from where they had been and put their arms around Bella.

'Don't cry Bella, we are all in this together and we will not leave you here.'

The 'silver soldiers,' paid no attention to the distressed kids but kept working on their computers.

At last, the large group approached the nine and they were thoroughly scrutinised by them. They seemed fascinated by Faith's hair and took turns touching and pulling it gently.

Finally, growing angry at all this touching, her temper blazed. 'Stop touching me! You are all extremely rude and ill-mannered. It is not allowed to touch a person without permission, you are VERY uncivilised!' She pulled away and stood behind Liam.

'Uncivilised? We are not allowed to touch?'

The nine all shook their heads together and chorused, "NOT ALLOWED".

Alfie stood tall with his chin out and told the aliens, 'You must NEVER touch anyone without their permission, everyone knows that.'

'Everyone knows that, except YOU ALIENS,' Nonie said, and Hughie nodded and said 'Yes, EVERYONE.'

The silver ones had nothing to say to this, but they did stop touching Faith's hair.

The nine were left alone now and crept over to a wall opposite the computers and sat down in a huddle.

'I think we have given them something to think about,' Bella grinned at them, some confidence beginning to return.

'They have never met humans before, obviously,' Liam commented. 'It must be strange for them too.'

'I think we should do something mad, to show them that they would be better off without us on board.' June ventured this idea.

'Like what, exactly?' Liam thought this was a crazy idea. 'Who knows how they might react?'

June said in an eager tone, 'let's entertain them! Bet they have never seen humans, or aliens for that matter sing and dance and make a darn great noise.'

'It would certainly make them very confused,' Bella said uncertainly.

'Okay, lads what do you suggest?' Rose looked at them all.

Nonie bit her lip, 'I suppose I could sing Knick-Knack -Paddywhack?'

'We need more than that, we need to keep this up for a while. Mira, you must do an Irish dance, then we will all get up and try and do an Irish dance, holding hands.'

'Don't be daft, none of you know how to.' Mira had to grin; it was pure madness.

'No matter just let's do it,' Liam said with authority. 'Hughie, Alfie and I will sit on the floor and beat out a rhythm with our hands. What do you say?'

'It's better than sitting and waiting for them to make the next move, I suppose.' Mira nodded.

'Okay, off you go Mira, you set it in motion.'

Liam started a drum-like beat with his hands on the floor and the boys followed his example.

Mira, taking a deep breath stood up. Facing the eight, she stood perfectly straight and pointed her toe and started to dance.

Chapter 18

Some seconds passed and then the boys drumming became louder and more insistent. Mira leapt and whirled and put her 'all' into the dance that she knew so well. The rest of the girls clapped in time to the drumming of the boys. Now and then they cried, 'Yay! Good on you, girl!'

Now they had an audience. The aliens stood facing the dancing girl and seemed to be paralysed. There was nobody tending to the computers now. They all stared intently at the dancing Mira.

'Guys, I'm running out of breath,' whispered Mira as she whirled by the group of girls. 'Time to get up and help me.'

The girls immediately rushed in, and taking each other by the hand, formed a circle and kept up the dancing although a bit slower. They made up the steps as they went along, sometimes tripping slightly and then laughing out loud at the madness of it all. The boys' hands were aching with all the drumming on the floor, so they started clapping instead and banging their feet hard on the floor.

They could not keep going forever and finally collapsed on the floor and laughed hysterically. The boys looked at each other uncertainly and then joined them.

The silver ones approached cautiously, 'what is all this? Why do you do such things?'

'It's what humans do,' Nonie said, but then erupted into laughter.

'Do you not dance?' asked Hughie, with a wide grin on his face.

'Dance? This thing is 'dance'? Why do you do such a thing?'

'You are NOT human, so you cannot understand.' Bella said, with a toss of her head.

'Every nation on earth knows how to dance, you don't know what you're missing,' Rose told the silent silver ones. 'It's a part of being civilised, you see.'

'We know nothing of this, but it seems strange,' the usual alien came closer. 'You make war on each other and dance?'

'We don't make war, and certainly not when we dance. Anyway, wars were in the olden days,' said June.

'Oh, not only in the past; even now, worse wars, worse weapons. You see, we understand a lot about your planet.'

'But you only see a small part of it,' argued Liam. 'You don't know about all the good things that happen on earth, do you?'

'It's enough that we know the bad things,' argued the alien. 'You do much to damage our worlds and we have many worlds, not just a small one like yours.'

This silenced the nine. How could they convince these aliens that they were innocent of harm?

'We must do strong things to stop your world from destroying ours, earthlings, otherwise, they will not listen to anyone. We must take strong action to deter your inhabitants from filling our space here with their rubbish.'

'What sort of strong things?' asked Hughie.

'If you are striking our planets and spaceships with dangerous objects, we must also send objects to collide with your earth and do some damage. Then maybe humans will think again about hurting us.'

This thought frightened the nine.

'You mean, like asteroids?' whispered Nonie.

'Like asteroids never seen before,' nodded the silver one.

Chapter 19

The nine sat on the floor in sad resignation. How could they convince these aliens of their innocence in all this. They thought quietly, sometimes turning to each other to express an opinion. Their heads were beginning to ache with all the thinking they were doing.

'We cannot do anything, can we,' moaned Nonie.

'No, there is nothing we can do to convince them to let us go.' Bella sighed deeply. 'I would never have left Australia if I knew this would happen.'

'Do you think that any of us would have left home for a holiday?' Faith was fed up.

'We must convince them that we are not valuable to them in any way at all,' decided Liam.

'How can we? We are only kids,' June said this with a wobble in her voice. She felt very sad; she was missing her parents of course, but also all her friends from school and her football club.

'They are so strong. Their bodies look like tinfoil and feel sort of soft, but the strength in their grip was painful,' Liam's arm still hurt.

They looked up suddenly as the alien group started moving towards them, leaving only a few at the computers.

'Now is time you must go back to other ship; you will stay,' one said, pointing at the four chosen.

'No, we are all cousins, you cannot separate us, that is cruel,' protested Faith.

'How do you think this will help you?' Belle asked this softly, she was about to burst into tears.

'When humans understand that we have hostages here, they will stop all experiments with rockets. They will want to get you back to earth, is this not so? We have learned that humans also use this method to get what they want.'

Liam stood up and faced the aliens. He took a deep breath and started what he hoped was a good explanation of human's understanding of space.

'What you do not understand, aliens, is this: no human on earth believes that you really exist. People laugh if you talk about the possibility of aliens existing in space. It's like us in Ireland; we talk about leprechauns, but we all know that they are not real.'

He paused to take another breath; he must make them understand before they started off again and separated them.

'If you really want them to believe that life exists in outer space by keeping some of us, well that will not convince them at all. But there is something you could do that would convince them and we could help you do that.'

The other eight looked at Liam with their mouths open. What was he talking about?

The aliens were listening and absorbing what Liam was saying.

'What is this way you can convince earthlings that we exist?'

Liam swallowed hard; he knew it was a crazy idea, but it was all he could think of.

'If you could let us have some of that material that you are made of? You see, I don't believe there is anything like that on earth, or else, *any* kind of material or metal, not found on earth.'

The aliens looked at each other.

'It's true,' Bella and Rose nodded. 'That is the only thing that might convince them, otherwise it would be like us telling them that there are leprechauns in space.'

At this Hughie, Alfie and Nonie got into a fit of hysterical laughter.

'Rusty doesn't look at all like a leprechaun,' giggled Nonie, and the boys howled with laughter at this.

The aliens did not laugh, well they probably never do, but they looked silently at the nine.

'Why do earthlings not believe we exist? We have given them many signs.'

'What sort of signs?' Liam was puzzled.

'We have given many sightings of spacecraft in the earth's atmosphere; many people must have seen them.'

'Oh, yes, I believe there have been sightings over the years,' Liam and Bella nodded at each other.

'But most people still don't believe in your existence, they need some solid, material proof,' Rose explained.

There was now silence and no movement from the aliens. The nine held their breath and prayed that this would convince the aliens that kidnapping them would not work at all.

Chapter 20

It seemed like a long time passed as the nine waited for a response from the aliens. First, the aliens all returned to their computers and typed furiously on their keyboards, surveying the screen in front of them continually.

Bella and Rose quietly moved up behind and tried to get a glimpse of a screen. They were most surprised to see a picture of a leprechaun on it, plus a lot of text they could not understand. It was not a language like theirs with their known alphabet, it was all funny signs and shapes they had never seen before.

They tiptoed silently back and told the others. Hughie and Alfie looked as though they were going to laugh again, but suddenly stopped as Liam held up his finger and glared at them.

'Not now. Don't dare laugh!'

'No, we must not make them angry or hostile, if we want to get off this ship,' Faith realised that there was a small chance they might now get away.

The aliens finally approached the nine again.

'What will the people on earth believe if four of you do not return? They must then believe that we exist, no?'

Liam tried to remain calm. 'They will simply believe that we did not survive the earthquake, or else, are just missing. They will think the other five are traumatised by their experience and have no memory of what happened.'

'What is wrong with your people on earth; why can they not believe? Are they so simple-minded? Do they believe in anything?'

'Of course they do,' Bella said. 'They believe in goodness, and truth and honesty.'

'Yes, and they believe in God too, that He made all this space stuff,' Hughie said rapidly, spreading his hands.

'And they believe that people can become anything they want, if they try hard enough,' Nonie had her say.

'Enough! We too of course know of the Great Spirit who creates all, but earthlings must learn their place in the order of things. They are only small and insignificant and have not yet learned where they fit in. Up to now, they destroy and pollute the earth, which cannot be allowed to continue, if not, they will start destroying and polluting all the universes.'

The silver one then folded his arms across his chest and stared at the nine.

'You are right of course,' Rose said softly. 'We all realise that the earth is being damaged by misuse and by the violence of some, but not all are like that. Honestly.'

'There are groups of people in every country that are trying to keep our oceans clean,' Mira said, looking around at them all.

'And what about all the countries trying hard to keep the forests alive and stop all this carbon emissions sort of business?' Hughie was trying desperately to recall all the conversations he had heard among his relatives about such things.

The silver one held up his hand. 'Enough! We know these things, but you must believe me when I say they are not trying hard enough. No, there is a metal too precious to them they must protect.'

'What do you mean? Which metal?' Faith was curious.

'You call it Gold, Precious Metals, Mon-ee, and Pro-fit, and all the nations on your earth care only for this.'

The nine had no answer to that; they knew everyone had to have money to exist and buy things.

'We do not have that much money,' protested June, 'we have to work to get pocket money,'

'Yes, my sister and I clean our granny's windows and do other jobs for her, for pocket money,' Faith looked at Mira, who nodded.

'Work is good, that is not the problem. The rich earth people want more and more, and it means some other people get less and less. Do you understand what I say?'

'Yes, we do, and you are right. That is called greed, and unfortunately it is part of our human nature,' Belle admitted sadly.

'We are not perfect, you know,' June protested hotly. 'I'm sure you are not either!'

'No, you are not perfect, that is truth, you have had lots of time, as you call it, to become perfect, but no, you prefer the other way, the imperfect way.'

Liam scratched his head. 'Well, that's how it is, so what will we do?'

'Only a big SHOCK will make it all change,' said the silver one, 'and that will come; you could perhaps warn them.'

Faith laughed out loud, 'do you think they will listen to children?'

'Only you will know, but you must try very hard to make them understand the danger they are in, not just a few, the whole planet.'

'How do you know all this?' asked Alfie, looking scared.

'It is easy for us, earthling, because it has happened before.'

'You mean the earth was destroyed before?' June was unconvinced.

'There were many earth planets before your present one, they all went the same way,' the silver one seemed to sigh, and his shoulders lifted and dropped again.

'Were you around when all that happened?' Nonie looked shocked.

'We were always here; safeguarding the many universes, we always will be.

Chapter 21

The nine could think of nothing more to say after they heard all this conversation. They sank down to the floor and tried to absorb all that the silver one said.

'They see themselves as the ones who guard the skies and all the planets and things in them,' muttered Bella in awe.

Nonie held her head in her hands. 'It's too much for my brain to understand,' she moaned softly. 'Will someone please tell me I'm in the middle of a nightmare and wake me up?'

Alfie patted her back, 'It's all true Nonie, but don't worry, I'm sure they won't want us. They don't like us earthlings very much, do they?'

The older ones had nothing to add and felt dismay and sorrow creep into their hearts. Would they ever get back to earth again? Would they ever see their parents again?

They were all crying silently, tears running down their cheeks, thinking about their lives before all this happened.

Then the silver ones were moving towards them once more. The nine stood up, preparing for the worst thing possible, separation.

'Earthling children must now return to other ship and depart.'

They looked at the one in front of them. He was standing holding out a sort of container.

Liam stepped forward and asked, 'can we all leave?'

'Yes, it has been decided you must all return to earth and tell your people that we do exist; you carry proof. You will not be separated this time.'

The nine all breathed a sigh of relief.

'Thank you, thank you,' they whispered softly.

'You will take this material and show the earthlings, it will surely convince them of our existence.'

Liam held out his hand and took the container.

'We will do our best, I promise you,' he said, in a steady voice. His heart was hammering madly as were all his cousins' hearts.

Then the door was opened automatically, and the canopy spread outward, connecting the two ships and the gangway was again moved into position.

Hardly daring to believe they were being freed, the nine walked carefully across. At last, they were all there and paused as they reached the safety of the first spaceship, then they each turned and gave a little wave to the silver ones who were now on the other side.

Then the doors of both ships closed, and the engines once again began to hum and they felt movement for the first time in ages, it seemed.

Their familiar aliens were all at the computers and did not pay too much attention to the nine.

They seemed to be punching in directions and codes and looking intently at the screens all the time.

The nine crept across the big room, found their bedroom and as one, they all fell on their beds and were fast asleep immediately, Liam clutching his parcel.

When they finally awoke, they felt fully refreshed for the first time in ages. How long were they on the other spaceship? There was no way of knowing. While there, they had felt no hunger, or sleepiness, which was strange.

Liam was curious to see what was in the parcel wrapped in strange material. The eight all crowded around to see the contents.

He took the strange metal object from the carton and there was also something else; a soft silver type of material that retained its shape even after it had been tightly squeezed.

'Ohh, this feels so strange.' Nonie liked the feel of this stuff; she had never felt anything like it before.

'Yeah, it's really soft isn't it.' Alfie liked it too.

'It's sort of springy.' Hughie took his turn feeling and squeezing it.

'What sort of metal is that.' Bella took the object which was quite heavy. It was black metal, shaped like a giant cigar.

I've never seen metal like that before; it's not steel. Maybe iron?' Liam weighed the object in his hand.

'Let's hope they know on earth,' suggested June.

Let's hope they don't, otherwise they will not believe we got it in space.'

'You're right Rose, they will not believe us if this is a common metal on earth,' Bella said, 'but just imagine if nobody there has ever seen stuff like this!'

'We'll be famous and probably be on the telly,' gasped Hughie.

'That's given me an idea,' said Mira; 'do you think our *normal* aliens could give us something too?'

'Maybe something different?' Nonie suggested. 'Then they would have to believe us, wouldn't they? You know what grownups are like!'

'Yes, we will ask them too. The more evidence we have, the better.' Liam was very pleased, it meant that their strange travels would not be in vain and would benefit the whole of mankind. Maybe.

Chapter 22

There was food in the dining room and the nine eagerly sat down to eat the usual Yucky double yucky stuff. Lone came in and stood by the door watching them. If an alien could look pleased to see them, then he did. Nonie gave him a little wave from where she sat, and he raised a stiffly bent arm in reply.

'Have you missed us, Lone?' Alfie grinned as he asked this. He was quite fond of the alien now, especially having met the silver soldiers.

'Were we gone a long time?' asked Nonie.

'Missed? What is this?' Lone moved nearer the table.

'It just means that while we were on the other spaceship, did you think about us?'

'Yes, I did; I was thinking that you would not return here. It is a good thing that you are here again.'

'You thought we would stay there?' Rose was shocked at the idea.

'I though that earthlings would be very interesting to those others' research and knowledge.' Lone looked at these strange creatures and wondered what sort of lives they had.

'But they gave their word that we would come back if you handed us over to them,' Liam said.

'We did not think all of you earthlings would be allowed to return here; only some.'

'Well, thank heavens that we did all return,' exclaimed Bella.

'Are we back on course, do you know?' Rose asked this as the spaceship seemed to be travelling fast again.

'We are on course, almost. The asteroid did some damage, and we need to fix before we enter earth's atmosphere, otherwise, BANG!' Lone clapped his hands together as he said this. He did not seem to notice the shocked faces of the nine kids.

Bella swallowed hard. 'Have you ever crashed before, Lone?'

'Not *our* ship, but many ships do, through meeting asteroids or foreign objects floating around our space.'

'What happens the travelers in the spaceships then?' Faith had visions of aliens floating around forever.

'They get destroyed too, if not picked up by nearby ship.'

The nine silently digested this news. Aliens could be destroyed! They had never imagined this could happen.

When they had finished eating, they followed Lone out to the main hall. The computers and machinery were now all whirring and buzzing away as normal.

Rusty and a group were in a different part of the ship silently surveying the big screen ahead of them. The nine headed in that direction.

They could see something that looked like the wing of a plane. A piece of it, like a panel, seemed to be flapping about and that did not look normal to them.

'I bet that's the damaged part,' whispered Liam to the others.

'How on earth will they fix that?' wondered Rose.

'Certainly *not* on *earth*,' said Faith with a giggle.

'What I meant is, surely it will be necessary to get outside the spaceship to secure it,' explained Rose.

They all looked at the flapping panel and knew she was right, unless of course, it could be done remotely from inside the spaceship.

Rusty turned away from the screen and saw the nine all standing looking worried.

'We have a problem, earthlings, you can see it, yes?'

They all nodded their heads.

'How are you going to fix that loose panel?' Liam pointed to the picture on screen.

'Can you fix it by remote control?' asked Mira.

'We have tried this, but it was not successful.'

Rusty turned back to the screen. 'The flap is the outer skin, but underneath are other layers that are also damaged and need to be pinned.'

'What are you going to do about it?' asked Faith, realising that even in space, problems had to be solved like broken things on earth.

'Can you go outside the spaceship and repair it from there, would that not be the answer?' Bella thought it would be a simple job.

'Our fingers are not made to bend too easily, and it will require special expertise. We may have to wait for others to come to our rescue, but that may not be for many long, long cycles.'

This was too disappointing! They understood 'cycles' to mean time. The nine kids had thought that they would be heading home soon. The idea of waiting about for ages was totally horrific. Suppose no help arrived for years?

Chapter 23

June had an idea. 'Could *we* not help? Our fingers are very bendy; after all, I play the violin and my sister plays the piano. Your fingers have to be very strong and bendy to do that.'

Rusty looked a bit confused, they thought.

'You think you can go outside and help?'

'Well, we can try, can't we?' Hughie felt very brave and wanted to help. It was a good way to get home fast.

Liam was pondering the difficulties involved. 'You would have to secure whoever goes out with a rope, otherwise they would just float away.'

The other eight looked at him in horror. Float away?

Rusty looked at him. 'We understand all about repairs outside ship, all this is possible for strong bendy fingers. You would try this?'

Now it was Liam's turn to feel sick with fright.

'How far from the main door is this part of the ship?'

'On the other side,' replied Rusty.

'How would we be able to find it?' asked Rose.

'Many lights would show the way,' Rusty said, 'we would also be in contact with you remotely and give you instructions on what to do.'

'How many people would it take?' asked Faith.

Rusty returned to view the screen. The nine crowded closer to him.

'Would need many strong bendy fingers, all working closely together.'

'We each have three very strong fingers on each hand, and two weaker ones,' said Rose.

'Let's show Rusty our fingers and let him decide who should go,' suggested Mira.

They all thought that this was a sensible suggestion and told Rusty that he must pick the strongest fingers among them. The three youngest were immediately ruled out as their fingers were small enough but not strong enough.

The fingers of the other six were examined carefully by several aliens and they all seemed to agree on their choice, after some time.

They waited nervously as the aliens looked at each other, busily communicating with their eyes.

Then Rusty came and picked Rose, Mira and June.

The three girls looked at one another and swallowed. 'Will it be safe, do you think?' June whispered.

Now everyone was worried stiff. What had they volunteered for, and would it succeed?

Mira was not too worried. 'Once they have a rope around us, we should be okay, they can haul us back in whenever.'

'Yes, I suppose so,' agreed Rose.

June just hoped they were right.

The aliens were now back at their screen and seemed to be agreeing about something.

Liam and Bella were frightened now.

'If you don't want to do it you can always refuse you know,' Bella said.

'I'm the tallest and strongest, I should really go,' said Liam. It was true; he was very tall and strong and played rugby.

'It's the fingers that are important,' Mira reminded them. 'Mine are used to doing crochet and that's quite difficult at times, using a small hook. Yours are too big, Liam.'

'Mine are very strong from all the scales and arpeggios I have to practice,' said Rose.

'Well, mine are quite nimble, although I don't practice my violin as much as I should,' said June.

'Well if you don't want to go June, I'll take your place,' Bella volunteered.

Rose reminded them that Rusty was the one who made the decision, and they must abide by that. After all, he was an experienced alien and knew what he was about.

Now there was a lot of activity about the ship. Three helmets of strange material were brought to the three and they had to try them on. The aliens seemed to think they were alright and then three sorts of funny suits were brought out for the girls to try on. They seemed a bit short in the legs to them, but the aliens were happy. There was a clear visor on top of the helmets which was lowered down over the girls' faces and they were examined again carefully by Rusty and the others.

Now the helmets were removed, and another group of aliens approached the girls and tied a metal belt around each waist. The girls watched as a strong metal chain was threaded through the buckles on each metal belt. This was secured with a type of lock; each waist band had two buckles. The chains connecting all of them were then measured out and seemed very long. The ends of the chains were then secured to a large metal handle attached to the wall at the side of the main door.

The nine surveyed this operation and wondered if it was really happening. They were in shock mostly, but not the three girls. They knew they must be fully alert, everything depended on *them* being able to do a difficult job.

Now the three were taken to one side and shown different tools and were given instructions as to what needed to be done. The other six were herded away to their consternation. Lone came into the dining room and explained.

'The three earthlings must remember all instructions and what each tool is for, it is thought that if you are all there too, it will be distracting for them. You understand?'

They were not sure they understood that. The enormity of what was about to happen was only now beginning to dawn on them.

Chapter 24

After what seemed like ages, the six cousins were summoned from the dining room by Rusty.

'It is time for earthlings to go and try and repair damage. Come! You will watch the progress on screen.'

They stumbled out and saw the three standing by the door, fully helmeted now and standing ready for the door to open.

The six did not know what to do. They tried to get close to the cousins but were not allowed by the group of aliens that surrounded them.

All they could do was to shout, 'TAKE CARE, STAY SAFE, LOVE YOU.....'

Alfie said in a small voice, choked with tears, 'I'll say a special prayer for you.'

'Your guardian angels will help you, lads.' Hughie said this in a strong voice, he was full of confidence that all would be well.

Nonie burst into tears and clung to Faith and Bella, both of whom looked like they wanted to howl too. Liam was white in the face and felt like he was going to be sick.

The door was fully opened and the three turned and waved to the other six, then they stepped outside and onto the platform, which was there, attached by a cable controlled by an alien on the main computer inside.

The six gathered around the big screen, trying to see what was happening. It took a while for the platform to be seen, being slowly manoeuvred around the spaceship until it had reached the damaged part.

They watched spellbound, hardly daring to breathe, as they watched the girls standing closely together to begin this vital work. They seemed to understand exactly what to do. June was holding the outside flap up with both hands and Rose, the under flap, while Mira leaning inwards, worked on the innermost part doing something with a spanner-like tool.

When she appeared finished, she gestured a thumbs up sign and waited. The alien at the main computer spoke into a gadget, attached to the computer that looked like a mobile phone and said in its robot-like voice, 'Mission accomplished earthling, now the second stage, please.'

The same procedure took place again and the middle flap was secured and finally the outer flap, held by June.

When the job was complete, the girls were informed by the alien and told to hold on to the platform rail as they were now being returned to the ship.

When they finally got back, and the door was shut behind them, the six rushed to them excitedly and helped the aliens to remove the helmets and outer clothing.

The excitement was mighty and even the aliens appeared exhilarated and happy, if you can describe it as that. They all crowded around the three, touching them and clapping their hands.

The three girls were exhausted, and their hands ached.

'What was it like,' the six wanted to know.

June laughed giddily, 'like nothing on earth.'

Mira was rubbing her hands as was Rose.

'Oh, it was so hard; just moving our fingers was so difficult, my hands are aching.'

'It was, and the flaps were heavy and so hard to keep up.' Rose said and June agreed.

'I was terrified I would drop the tool at first, but once I began, I just told myself to concentrate.'

'It looked so easy, watching you on the screen, it did not look difficult at all,' Bella said.

'If we had known how difficult it would be, we might not have volunteered,' said Rose and the other two agreed with her.

Rusty came up and all the aliens formed a circle around the nine.

'Earthlings! We are all very grateful for your assistance. It was serious damage to our ship, and we might not have been able to travel far again. You have proved superior in this repair work to us.'

After this speech all the aliens clapped their hands and made strange humming sounds.

The nine gratefully returned to the bedroom and while the three girls who had been outside repairing, fell fast asleep immediately, the other six lay quietly talking about everything that had happened to them.

'Do you think we will be able to return to earth now?' whispered Alfie.

'I don't see why not,' answered Liam.

'It should be full steam ahead,' said Faith, happily.

Chapter 25

Alfie and Hughie were looking out of the portholes in the dining room. It was like watching a film in a cinema. The stars rushing by them and the other objects slowly moving either away from them or towards them were fascinating to watch. Sometimes they ducked their heads, thinking that an object was about to come into the dining room.

'I thought that was going to hit us,' gasped Hughie, standing up again.

'It was probably miles away. They look as though they are very close, don't they?'

'How long do you think we have been here, Alfie? We could be already a few weeks away from home.'

'It seems like weeks, but the important thing is, how long will it be before we are home again?' Alfie sighed and turned away from the porthole.

Nonie came out and joined them and the three moved into the computer room, where they soon cornered Lone at his computer.

'Do you have any games to play here, Lone?' Nonie looked pleadingly at the alien.

'Games? Explain this word.'

'Games are things we play to keep us from being bored.' Hughie thought that this explained the word 'games' very well.

'Bored?' Explain this word.

Oh no, this would take ages, the three all thought.

Nonie tried her best as the boys looked at each other, rolling their eyes.

'Do you ever have nothing to do, Lone? You know, when everyone else is busy and you are not busy. Do you not feel empty because you have nothing to do?'

'Always we are busy, never without work,' Lone looked at her. 'See, this is my workplace here, everyone has their own workplace.'

'Well, you were not all working when your ship was damaged, were you?' Alfie said with a grin.

'Yes, you all stopped working when our cousins had to go outside to repair the damage.' Hughie said triumphantly.

'It was a bad time, waiting for repair to be finished,' Lone agreed.

'Do you never play games with each other,' Hughie asked with despair in his voice.

'We are all bored and need to do things; you work all the time; we work but we also play.' Nonie hoped Lone could understand the difference she was trying to explain.

'When we go to different planets and make landing, we sometimes take learning skills; you know we must learn all about different developments. There are many changes in our universes, and we must understand them, our worlds are expanding always; nothing stays the same.'

'Really? That's confusing. I'm glad our world stays the same,' Alfie said.

'The seasons change though,' said Hughie.

'The climate is changing too,' Nonie said thoughtfully, 'in fact I've heard people say that parts of earth will not be habitable if it continues because there will be lots more wildfires.'

'Yep, the seas will get higher and swallow islands, because the ice caps are melting,' Alfie nodded, and a worried look came over his face.

'The land will get too hot for people to live in, and the seas will be too hot for the poor fish,' Hughie bit his lip. 'Imagine that!'

Liam and the others had come up behind the three and had heard this conversation.

'Don't get all down in the dumps lads, that's why we have scientists doing research and learning about how to stop it.'

'Our sister Joey is learning all about space. She will know if there is a planet like our world, where we can go and live on, if things get too bad on earth.'

'Yes Hughie, but she will have to hurry up, bad things are happening already,' Alfie said sadly.

Lone stopped working on his computer and turned to the nine earthlings. 'Many good planets like earth, you understand. Many, many.'

'Wow, is that really true, Lone?' Bella was amazed.

Mira had an idea. 'If things got really bad on earth and humans could no longer live there, would you come and rescue us and bring us somewhere else?'

'Yes, like to another earth-like planet where we could live safely?' June thought this was a great idea.

Lone surveyed the nine for a minute. 'If you destroy earth then you will destroy wherever you go; you must learn not to destroy. Earthlings take cycles and cycles to understand and still, they to not know how well-balanced the earth must be to survive.'

'How do you mean, well-balanced?' queried Nonie.

'All must be in harmony, nature and human life. All must be treated with respect and looked after, do you understand all this?'

The nine did and they also understood how much their earth was hurting from not being looked after.

After this conversation they returned to the dining room and sat around the table to play guessing games to try and stop thinking about the state the earth was in.

Chapter 26

Time passed and the nine kids lost track of everything; the sound of the computers and the feeling of movement dulled their senses.

Lone appeared at intervals to announce Yucky double yucky. Then they would drag themselves off their beds and go to the dining room to eat the usual food.

Liam approached Rusty to ask if they could have something from their spaceship that would convince the people of earth that there was life outside. Rusty said he would consider it.

Then in one of their sleeping moments, there was a jolting movement and all nine were catapulted from their beds.

'Oh no! Not another earthquake,' moaned Alfie.

They scrambled to their feet, and all went to the hall where the aliens were at their computers.

Did they ever leave them, they wondered. They obviously did not need rest like humans.

'What is happening Rusty? Have we been hit again by asteroid or maybe a meteorite?' Liam looked at the screen but could see little to enlighten him.

'No, it is because we have entered earth's atmosphere and it's very different to before.'

'Wow! Does that mean we will be home soon?' Rose felt excited and fully awake now.

'We have to get on the right course for earth, we have to proceed carefully, or we may miss and go in the wrong direction, there are many things pulling our ship, this way and that way, like currents in the atmosphere.'

The nine looked at Rusty and the other aliens with respect. What did *they* know about all these things. What sort of dangers were there, and could they miss the earth?

'How long will it take, do you think,' whispered Faith.

'We will know when we see the blue planet clearly.'

'Gosh! I never would have believed it was so complicated,' said June.

'It is better if you go back and rest. You may get fearful if you stay.' Rusty pointed to the door and the nine knew they must obey.

Off they trooped and tried to rest on their beds and not worry. Sleep was impossible now. It seemed to them that the spaceship twisted and turned a lot, and it was bumpy.

'It's just like when we were on that plane. Do you remember how bumpy it was?' Nonie was afraid again.

'That's when we hit pockets of air, I think,' said Liam.

'Let's hope we don't crash land,' said Alfie. 'I don't fancy another hike through a jungle.'

'If the aliens were able to land safely before, while there was an earthquake, I'm sure they'll do it again.' Rose said confidently.

'Let's hope the earthquake is finished,' muttered Hughie.

'Of course, it is. We've been gone weeks, if not months. Earthquakes last only hours, I think.' June said, secretly praying that she was right.

'Can you imagine the excitement when we arrive home? Everyone will be so happy.' Nonie was getting ready for the great reunion.

'I bet there will be a big party to welcome us home,' smiled Faith.

'There will be a lot of people from the media and television, I would think,' Hughie was imagining the attention they would all get, after all, it had never happened before, had it? An alien abduction!

'They did not really abduct us tho', did they?' Nonie looked at them all. 'They were really only rescuing us, don't you think?'

That set them all thinking hard. Abduction or rescue, which was it?

'That's a difficult question,' Liam said.

'I think they were just in the area at the time, and it suited them to take us for their research.' Bella said.

'Yeah, they're not really bad guys at all,' declared Alfie. 'They know a lot about the earth.'

Suddenly there was silence all around them and they could no longer hear the computers. It felt like the spaceship was no longer moving.

Nine faces all got a bit pale and stared at the door of their bedroom. Where were they? Had they landed back on earth?

Chapter 27

It was Rusty who came to the bedroom door, then entered the room.

The nine held their breath and looked at him expectantly.

'Earthlings, we have landed on earth, you are back home.'

At once a cheer arose from the nine and they danced around hugging each other and then clapping their hands.

'Well done, Rusty! You are a great alien.' They all shouted joyfully.

Rusty held up his hand, 'one problem,' he said, and the nine stopped where they were, suddenly silent.

'What is it, Rusty, what is the problem?' Liam was scared now, scared of the unknown.

Rusty explained in his robotic voice, 'we are not in same place where we found you, this place is different, but it is earth.'

They looked at one another. This was not a big problem. The important thing was that they were back on their own planet, weren't they?

Rusty explained when spaceships approach earth, they must do so at night and avoid air space used by planes. One of their ships was shot down once, when they were in the wrong place. When the earthquake happened, it was at night, and they saw the seismic happening on their radar.

'So, what's the problem Rusty? We will find our way home, don't worry.'

'This is a problem earthling Nonie,' we are not sure if where we land is a good place or a hostile place for you. We know there are wars in various places on earth; they show up on our intelligence information.'

The nine considered this in silence. What if they had landed in Ukraine or in North Africa where there was fighting and bombing, or in the troubled Middle East.

Bella was the first one to voice their fears. 'This is all true, I'm afraid. We could be walking into a worse nightmare than the one we've been in.'

'Is there no place safe to land on earth?' Alfie sounded upset and angry too.

'We must first try and find out where we are, then you will know how near your place is.' Lone had crept up to stand beside Rusty.

'But you said we've landed; does that mean you may have to take off again?' Faith was so confused and disappointed.

'We will send out probes, as we call them, and try to pick up any information we can about this place. It may take a while longer before you can leave spacecraft. No problem!' Rusty seemed to think that this would satisfy the disappointed kids.

Lone moved closer to them. 'You can help us too; you will hear what we hear and if you recognise the language spoken, then you will know where you are. We know there are many different languages spoken on earth, not like us in space.'

They all followed the two aliens into the computer room and gathered around the biggest screen. Although it looked very dark outside, it appeared to the older kids that they were high on a mountain, with smaller mountains on all sides.

They peered intently at the screen, hoping to identify where they were.

'It doesn't look like anything I've seen before,' muttered June.

'It's so dark, how can we tell?' Rose said.

'Maybe we're in the Himalayas,' joked Hughie and immediately got a poke in his side from Nonie.

'It's not a joking matter, this is really bad.' Liam was scratching his head. 'It could be the Himalayas and then how would we ever survive, never mind find our way home?'

Mira remained calm and cool. 'Let's not get bogged down with bad thoughts. Let the aliens do their probing and if they find no signs of civilisation or hostile ones, we can take off again and try somewhere else.'

That sounded like the most sensible idea to all of them. Better to be safe than sorry was the thought in the nine heads.

Chapter 28

They were once again flying in space. The probe had not shown anything in the vast area that was probed, nothing at all.

The aliens were now working flat out to change their direction and the screens were throwing up maps and charts of all sorts on the various screens.

The younger cousins soon crept off to bed and were soon in a deep sleep. The older ones stayed watching the screens and praying something good would soon happen.

'You speak Eng-leesh only, yes?' One of the aliens was consulting his screen and comparing it to a chart on another screen.

'Yes, and Irish too, 'cos we're Irish.' June helped out.

The alien peered at his screen, 'not Jap-an-ese?'

'No, for sure, not Japanese.' Liam said.

'Mind you, I would love a big sushi meal right now,' muttered Faith.

'It'd be a long walk home,' remarked Mira.

'Don't dare talk about food, we have not had Yucky double yucky for ages,' moaned Rose.

Lone immediately picked up on that.

'You come now, there is Yucky double yucky stuff for you in dining room.'

They moaned when they heard that; they had thought those meals were a thing of the past.

All but Liam and Bella left for the dining room.

They listened as they heard the aliens say in their robotic voices, names of places they had never even heard of and a few that they had.

'Azerbaijan', 'Mongolia', 'Djibouti', 'Siberia'....
It went on and on, and the two cousins wondered when they would hear of some country that they were familiar with. It was depressing but also scary.

Soon the others returned and started watching again.

'You should really eat something,' Rose told Liam and Bella, 'we don't know how long this will be.'

'Yes, you've got to keep your strength up, if we have to walk any distance when we do get off the ship.' Faith advised them and Mira agreed.

Reluctantly Liam and Bella left to go to the dining room.

Now they could see the sun rising on their part of the world and the spaceship seemed to accelerate away into the darkness again. They felt disappointment and tiredness creeping up on them again. Shortly afterwards they walked slowly to the bedroom and slept along with the younger three.

Much later they awoke and lay quietly, thinking about the newest problem facing them. Would they ever find their parents and where on earth were they?

When they returned to the computer room, Rusty left his screen and went up to the nine.

'What name of country was earthquake?'

'Italy,' they all replied.

'Italy your home country?'

'No, we were on holidays in Italy. Ireland is where we live,' said Rose.

Bella was going to say that she was Australian but decided that it might complicate matters. If she could get to Ireland safely, she could then get to Australia.

'Holidays? That is visit, yes?' asked Rusty.

'Yes, earthlings travel a lot around the world on holidays, but we always go home afterwards.' Faith said, tossing her red hair.

Chapter 29

It was not long after this conversation that the aliens suddenly began to get agitated, or excited, it seemed to the nine.

They drew near the big screen where Rusty was pointing with his finger and then at other maps of screens.

'Many rivers and mountains in your country?' he asked.

'Yes many, Rusty.' They hardly dared to breathe.

'We are going to hover for a while and send out electrical probes. If technology nearby we will hear,' explained Rusty.

They waited with bated breath and prayed silently that they were near home, at last.

'This is good earthlings; we are getting transmissions from this place, and they are in Eng-leesh.'

They all clutched each other in excitement.

'But maybe other countries speak Eng-leesh?'

Oh no! Why did he have to put a dampener on this good news.

'It doesn't matter, does it?' Nonie pleaded.

'People will know what we are talking about, we'll find out way back,' Hughie was full of confidence.

'If it's in America, it might take a long time,' Alfie reminded them.

'Right, and they might treat us as illegal immigrants too and lock us up!' Faith moaned.

'Oh, shut up Faith! Why look on the dark side of things. Do you want to be hovering everywhere forever?' June was getting annoyed.

'Look, Faith has a point, lads, we don't want to end up in a worse position, do we?' Mira said.

'Rusty, can you listen to some of the conversation so that we can be sure of where we are?' Liam hoped that this was possible.

Rusty nodded and said, 'we will try and get clear transmission from earthlings here.'

The answer came through shortly after this. The transmission was put on the highest volume, and they all heard it clearly. It was a radio broadcasting the latest sports news.

"Tomorrow evening, Kerry faces Dublin in the All-Ireland Hurling Championship here in Croke Park....."

The nine started cheering and shouting in joy and the rest of the transmission was lost in the noise.

The nine could not believe it; it seemed they were over Ireland and their relief and joy overflowed.

They grabbed the alien nearest them and threw their arms around them, danced them around the floor, much to the astonishment of the aliens!

Then it was back to the computers, and they felt the spaceship begin to descend quite sharply.

Rusty pointed to the nine to return to the other room and they went happily. They picked up their backpacks which they had not worn for a long time. Liam carefully packed his precious memento from the other spaceship.

When all movement and sound ceased, Rusty came into the dining room and announced that they had landed safely.

'Earthlings are happy to leave now?' he asked.

'Oh, yes, Rusty. If we are in Ireland, we are home and safe.' Bella said.

The others all agreed loudly and began to thank Rusty and Lone who appeared behind him.

Lone handed Liam a packet.

What is this Lone, a goodbye present?' he asked.

'Yucky double yucky stuff; you will be hungry?'

The nine cousins all yelled loudly, 'Oh, thank you Lone, thank you very much.'

Rusty then handed Bella a smaller parcel wrapped in a soft wrapping.

'You need proof for earthlings? This is proof, this not found on earth.'

The door was opening and even though they were excited about leaving they felt a bit of sadness at saying goodbye to these creatures who had, after all, rescued them at the time of the earthquake and were not in the least harmful to them.

Rose stepped forward and held out her hand. As Rusty did not seem to know what was expected, she took his hand and shook it gently.

'Thank you Rusty and Lone and all you other aliens. We are grateful that you have brought us home.'

Rusty said in that strange voice, 'we will always be watching over earth and when you need help, we will rescue you again.'

Then it was time to step out of the spaceship and try to find out where exactly they were. But this time, they were confident and happy, and they all turned to wave at the watching aliens as they walked away into the night.

Chapter 30

After a few yards stumbling along an uneven path, they turned to see the spaceship ascending gently, all the lights gradually getting dimmer, and then it was no more.

The silence around them enveloped them and they tried to see any sign of human habitation, but all was dark. Then suddenly a wonderful thing happened, the moon came out from behind the clouds and now they could see more clearly.

They were on a level patch of ground but there were stones and rocks all over the place.

'Be careful, lads, watch your step,' called Bella, who led the way, followed by Rose and Mira. June and Faith held the young boys' hands and Nonie walked in front of them with her brother Liam.

They were surrounded by tall trees and no lights could be seen anywhere. They were not worried at all. This was Ireland.

Now they were climbing, and the ground was rockier, and they had to slow down. Then as they rounded a bend on their left, they suddenly saw outlined against the sky, a large cross.

They stopped in amazement.

'I think we are on top of a mountain,' cried Hughie, excitedly.

They trudged forward faster. Now and then the clouds would cover the moon but after a while it would come out again and seemed to shine more brightly than ever.

Now they were almost at the foot of the cross and turning around they found themselves speechless. They knew where they were!

'I've been here before,' said Liam in a loud voice. 'We're in Bray! This is Bray Head!'

Hughie shouted 'Halleluiah,' although he had never been to Bray.

'Are you sure? asked Bella, as she had never been either.

'Yes, yes! We were on holiday here a few years ago and had a great time,' shouted Faith.

'We sure did,' Rose laughed.

'A very adventurous time,' added June.

'We joined you then, didn't we? Hughie asked, 'but not in Bray.'

'You did, Hughie, further down the coast.'

They looked happily down and could see the lights of Bray twinkling in the distance, the sea moving gently backwards and forwards.

Oh! This was better than they could have hoped for. They had relatives in Bray.

They continued carefully down the mountain; it was quite steep and unfamiliar. The last time they were here, Liam's father and Mira and Faith's father had challenged each other to a race down the mountain. It had ended badly with lots of bruises.

They wondered what time of night it was.

'Will we ever get used to looking at our watches again?' asked Faith.

'Well, we survived without knowing the time, didn't we? June replied.

'We don't even know what day it is,' Alfie said.

'Have we missed any birthdays, I wonder,' mused Nonie.

'We might all be years older now.' Hughie laughed.

'Yeah, just imagine if we turn up the same as before and our parents have all turned into old people.' June laughed too; it was such a funny idea.

'Don't laugh! It's not a funny idea at all,' warned Mira. 'Remember we have been in a place where time does not exist; anything might have happened here that we know nothing about.'

That quietened them all. They had once had a strange experience of being brought back in time and although it was nearly forgotten now, old fears and feelings again surfaced.

Nobody spoke after this, and they were soon at the base of Bray Head and could see clearly now the lit-up promenade and could smell the lovely salty smell of the sea.

Chapter 31

There was both rejoicing and bewilderment among the two adults when the nine were found standing on their doorstep.

They were delighted to discover the nine were alive and well but puzzled as to how they had found their way there, to Bray, of all places.

'Where are your parents, why are you not with them.? That was the big question that the nine could not answer.

Liam asked if he could ring his parents' mobile numbers to find out where they were. There was no answer. Then Mira tried her parents' number and again, no answer.

At this Nonie burst into tears, followed by Hughie and Alfie.

The adults did their best to comfort them. They told the children their parents were all alive and everyone in Ireland knew about the earthquake in Matera. They explained to the kids that there was a lot of confusion in the area and searches were still going on. Their parents were all safe in a place in France where efforts were being made to reunite families parted by the earthquake.

The nine were then offered a shower followed by a meal and then a nice bed. They were told that while they rested, the authorities would be notified about their safety.

The nine were so weary and footsore that they did not argue but happily accepted everything.

As they all sat, nice and clean, in borrowed clothing, eating a wonderful meal of chicken and chips, they smiled at each other. This was the most delicious meal ever.

The next morning it took a while for them to realise where they were. They all trooped downstairs to the kitchen where the cousin of their parents was preparing breakfast.

'Sit down lads and I'll have a lovely breakfast ready very soon.'

'Thank you so much Jenny, you have been great. We were not even sure we had the right house.' Rose had not met Jenny more than a couple of times in the past.

'Where are your children, Jenny? Liam asked, 'you have two, don't you?'

'Yes, a boy and a girl, both at school right now.'

'Oh! That means we have been missing school. What month is it, Jenny?' Faith asked.

It's November and school began yesterday after the midterm break. Our two were in bed when you arrived as they were exhausted after the first day back.'

'November!' They looked at each other in disbelief. They had gone to Italy the last week of August.

They busied themselves then with the beautiful breakfast put before them.

They were so busy eating that they did not see the two gardaí enter the kitchen at first.

'Oh wow! That was scrummy,' said Hughie, wiping his mouth on his napkin.

'After Yucky double yucky stuff, everything is scrummy.' Alfie smiled at them all.

Then they caught sight of the policemen and stopped, puzzled.

'Have you found our parents?' Liam asked.

'They are being contacted as we speak, we just have a few questions about how you arrived here; who brought you here?'

The two gardaí sat themselves down at the table and Jenny placed a pot of tea in front of them.

'Well, now lads. Everyone is delighted you all survived that awful 'quake, and your parents too. We just are a bit puzzled as to how you managed to get here, you know? Your parents have your passports, they told us.'

The older cousins knew that this was going to be a bit tricky and wondered how best to convince them of their weird travels in space.

Before anyone could answer, Hughie burst out excitedly: 'we were all abducted by aliens, in fact, two different groups of aliens…'

Alfie butted in, 'yes, and we've been in a faraway space place, much further than earth.'

'They rescued us on the beach after the earthquake and we didn't know it was a spaceship until later,' explained Nonie.

One garda looked at the other and both smiled slightly.

'Ah yes, I see. You were abducted by aliens and were in space for all this time?'

'We are not sure about the time, because you see, up there they don't have time,' said June.

'But how did you come to arrive in Bray?'

Nobody answered until Liam plucked up courage and told them.

'The aliens landed the spaceship at the back of Bray Head, and we walked down. We knew where to find Jenny's house, roughly.'

The two guards looked at Liam, then at each other, before starting to roar with laughter.

Chapter 32

There was silence in the kitchen as they all studied the two laughing men. Eventually they stopped laughing and looked at the nine serious faces in front of them.

'We do have proof, you know,' Bella said hotly, 'we are not making this up.'

'No, of course not. You have been through a very traumatic experience, and everyone will understand your confusion, don't worry.'

When the guards left, the nine sat in silence, feeling a bit dejected and subdued. They had of course suspected that no one would believe them, but still it hurt.

Jenny was great and passed no remarks nor asked any questions about anything. Instead, they all went for a brisk walk along the promenade and breathed in the fresh salty air deeply.

They were alone again that afternoon while Jenny went to collect her children.

Rose, Mira, Bella and Liam were huddled together talking very quietly. June and then Faith joined them and asked them why they were whispering together.

'It's just that we are worried.' Liam explained.

'Why? Soon we will be reunited with Mum and Dad; what are you worried about?'

Bella put up her hand and began to explain.

'We have proof, but we must be very careful who we give it to. Can you imagine if we had handed it over to the policemen this morning?'

June shook her head, mystified.

'Well, it could just end up in a drawer somewhere and never be scientifically examined.' Rose looked at her sister and June understood immediately.

'Gosh! We must be very careful who we give the proof to, don't we?' she asked.

Liam thought he had the answer. 'As soon as we are home, we must get in touch with Joey and ask her advice; what we have is of great importance to the world, remember.'

'We're hardly likely to forget the warning the silver soldiers gave us, are we?'

'More like threats, they were,' muttered Faith.

'We cannot afford to ignore them tho',' Rose said.

The nine were happily reunited with their parents, a couple of days later. The media also got wind of the safe arrival of the earthquake victims and wanted to interview them. They were both relieved and happy that something prevented this happening. It seemed that the press was not allowed anywhere near the nine and they were left in peace. They had no idea who made this happen, but it made the parents all wonder what had happened to the nine and they could hardly wait to get home to find out.

'You mean you were on the beach the same time as we were all running around looking for you?'

'Mum it was chaotic there, in the dark, screams and shouting. It was awful,' Mira explained to her mother.

'And you really believe you were abducted by aliens?' Liam's father Eamon looked at his only son with startled eyes. Who could believe this story.

'And the silver soldiers were not very nice; measuring us and making notes about us,' Hughie told his mum.

'They don't even understand feelings! Would you believe that?' Alfie was quite indignant.

'We had to explain loads of things to them,' Faith said. 'They did apologise to me for touching my hair without permission.' She nodded as she remembered her annoyance.

The parents all looked at each other. They knew their children; they could not make this up. The stories were amazing.

Then Liam produced his proof from the silver ones and from the other aliens as well.

That did it! The parents had never seen anything like this.

Bella then told them all why they were worried about who would get the proof.

'If it gets taken by a greedy person or anyone who wants to have control of it, then we must hold back and not let it leave us.' She looked at her parents anxiously, hoping they would understand.

'Yes, quite!' said her father, wondering what on earth they were getting into. To have escaped unharmed from an earthquake and now have this mystery hanging over them, it was unnerving!

'It's time we all returned to our own homes, and we won't mention it again until Joey comes home. She may be able to throw some light on the metals and stuff you have brought.' Liam's Dad spoke on behalf of all the parents.

'Will they still want to know how we came home, Dad?' asked Nonie.

'Maybe, but maybe not. It might be all hushed up.' He looked at the other parents and they nodded.

'Let's hope it is,' said Mira's mother.

'What about the warning we were giving? We can't hush up about that,' said Rose.

'I think we will all be getting a visit from some important people shortly, for each of your versions.' Mossie, the father of Hughie and Alfie said.

'For now, I think we should put the objects you were given in a secure place, just in case' Eamon said.

'Dead right, Dad,' said Liam, 'this stuff could be very dangerous in the wrong hands.'

'Maybe you could write down your memories while they are still fresh in your minds and leave out nothing, right?' Hughie and Alfie's mum had worked in journalism and radio a long time ago.

'Do I have to write about the awful Yucky double yucky stuff?' Alfie asked the others.

The others all dissolved into a fit of laughter.

'Of course, Alfie, you must.'

Printed in Great Britain
by Amazon